Finding Faith

The Diaries of the Woodsmall Sisters

Book One ~ Carolyn's Diary

Written by

Rachel E. Rittenhouse

Illustrated by

Autumn J. Detweiler

Finding Faith

The Diaries of the Woodsmall Sisters: Book One

Rachel E. Rittenhouse

Copyright © 2014 Rachel E. Rittenhouse

Published: April 2014
Cover Artist: Steven Plummer
Edited by: Tracy Seybold
ISBN-10: 1495948501
ISBN-13: 978-1495948503

This book is dedicated to

All the young girls I babysit for--Olivia, Elyse, Sophia,

Cecelia, Selah, Rachel, Heidi, Ashlyn, and Sarah--

So that they will have good Christian books

To read when they grow up.

And to my parents, John and Janelle,

Who have helped me along through

The writing, editing, and publishing process.

Enjoy!

Rachel E. Rittenhouse

Season 1

June 15, 1854

Dear Diary,

My name is Carolyn Faith Woodsmall. Today, for my 13th birthday, Momma gave me this diary to write in, because when I grow up, I want to be a writer. I have long, brown hair that shimmers when the sun hits it and dark brown eyes like Poppa.

I live with Poppa and Momma, my older brother Jesse, and my two younger sisters, Bethany and Laura. We

1

live on a farm in Minnesota. My Uncle Levi, Aunt Maria, and cousins Herb, Luke, and Kirsten live right next door. Well, almost next door. They live about half a mile to the west of us.

Being that today is my birthday, I received a couple of other presents in addition to my diary. Aunt Maria made me a new dark pink dress with roses on it, Kirsten made me a patchwork apron, Bethany and Laura made me a new dress and apron for my rag doll Wendy, Jesse and my oldest cousin Herb got me a quill and ink set, and Luke made some dishes for Wendy out of clay. But the best thing of all (besides my diary), Poppa and Uncle Levi got me a pony! Can you believe that! A real live pony! I was so shocked, Bethy said I was speechless. I have decided to name her Lucia after my favorite holiday in Sweden, St. Lucia's Day.

Over four years ago, my family left Sweden along with Momma's brother and his family (Uncle Levi). I was nine years old and I still remember some of the Swedish language. Grandpa and *Mormor* Cradle, Grandpa and *Farmor* Woodsmall, and many of my other aunts, uncles, and cousins still live there. Sometimes, I still imagine what it must be like to live there and I miss them all dreadfully. *Mormor* and *Farmor* both write letters pretty regularly as well as my cousin Millie Woodsmall. Millie, Kirsten, and I were best friends

2

when we lived in Sweden. We still are, but in a different way now. Now, letters must suffice our longings, for Uncle Amos (Millie's father) has said numerous times that he doesn't plan on moving to America.

June 16, 1854

Dear Diary,

Our schoolhouse is about one and a half miles north of us. Boys and girls, ages 4-15, attend school from October to April--the winter term. Then, boys and girls, ages 4-13, attend school from April to August--the summer term. Our teacher for the summer term is Mr. Crowl. He is pretty nice, but he is strict enough to keep the rowdy boys in line.

After school today, Kirsten, Farren Small (our best friend), and I went to a fort/playhouse in the woods. We have a little house that fits us if we sit down, and we made little furniture for our dolls as well as dishes. We don't really play anymore, just hang out and talk. Sometimes we will work on our schoolwork together.

June 17, 1854

Dear Diary,

After school today, Momma enlisted my help to make bread while she worked on supper. I always enjoy spending time in the kitchen with Momma. She always tells me stories about when she was younger and what she learned from her experiences.

Today, Momma told me about when she went out with her friends when she was younger and lost track of time. She was very late in returning home and had forgotten to tell her momma where she went. When she got home, her parents were very worried about her and scolded her. After the story, Momma said, "Always be responsible and keep track of time, Carolyn. There is no sense in worrying those who love you if you could've prevented it." Momma's stories and words of wisdom always stay with me for the rest of the day and a while after that. If only I could be as half as wise as Momma.

June 19, 1854

Dear Diary,

This morning, Momma sent Bethy and I to the woods to find some herbs she can use for cooking. I'm not a big outdoorsy type of girl, but the woods at this time of the year are so beautiful and I always have a good time with Bethy.

As we were walking, we came across Sherry and Cole Brown, who live on the other side of the woods. Sherry is my age and is, what some might call, a bully. That word might be a bit harsh, but she always seems to think she is better than us because her ancestors date way back to the Revolutionary War, while we just moved to America. Cole is closer to Jesse's age and he pretty much thinks along the same lines as his sister. He just ignores us girls.

When we passed them on the path, they almost pushed Bethy and I off. From behind us, I heard Sherry say, "There are those Swedish girls again. Who do they think they are waltzing through our woods?" I turned my head around to watch, and Sherry leveled me with an even stare. These are everyone's woods; how dare she say that? Bethy, our little peacemaker, gently pulled me away and we continued our search for Momma's herbs.

June 20, 1854

Dear Diary,

Today being Sunday, Poppa hitched up the wagon

and we rode over to the schoolhouse for church service. Reverend Mast preached about how we ought to trust God with everything, even when the impossible comes along. God can make all things possible, even if it doesn't seem like it.

After church, there is usually a potluck dinner and then we leave for home. I usually like to sit and write in the afternoon, because when I grow up, I want to be a famous *forfattare* (writer). What I am writing now is a book about my family's journey from Sweden and all the adventures and heartache we faced. I'm trying to keep it a secret though to surprise my family. Momma will be so pleased! I'm thinking about giving it to her on her birthday, which is November 16th. If I do that, I have lots of writing to do between now and then.

June 21, 1854

Dear Diary,

School was very enjoyable today. I do so love going to school. We are learning history, geometry, reading, arithmetic, and Bible. In history, we are learning about the American Revolutionary War. It is very interesting, and I love learning about it. The only problem is, at recess, Sherry flaunted around the whole playground, saying how her great-grandfather was a Patriot and how his store was burned by the Tories and so on, and so on. Kirsten and I were standing a ways off, just watching her. When she turned and saw us, she said in a loud voice, "Of course, some here have just come from a poor country across the ocean and probably sided with England!" I couldn't believe her. How could she say such things? We weren't even born yet! Bethy was by my side. "Turn the other cheek," she gently whispered. How could it be that my little sister is more patient than I?

June 23, 1854

Dear Diary,

Supper tonight was potato leek soup. So while I peeled the potatoes, Momma diced up the leeks really fine and told me another story.

"Did I ever tell you about the time I met your Aunt Maria?"

"No, I don't believe you have," I answered.

"Well, one summer day, my momma, *Mormor*, sent Levi and I into town to pick up some thread she needed for a shirt for Poppa. Levi did not want to go in the worse way and

I was anxious to return to my pie-making. You can just imagine, we were quite the pair; walking as fast as possible without actually running, with scowls on our faces. Quickly, I bought the thread and we headed home. On our way, Levi thought it would be a good idea to unravel some of the thread to see how long it actually was. I disagreed with him, but only because we disagreed on everything and not because I thought the idea was crazy. But he unraveled it anyways, though I don't know why he didn't listen to me, for I was the older one.

"A gust of wind suddenly came up and whipped the thread right out of our hands. Levi and I took off after our blowing thread, determined to reach it before something happened to it. In that stage of life, I was a faster runner than Uncle Levi. I was so intent on reaching that thread that I didn't see anyone in front of me. Levi screamed something at me, and I turned my head toward him and ran smack into someone, knocking us both to the ground. Rolling over, I saw that I had landed on a girl about my age, perhaps a little younger. Quickly standing up, I apologized numerous times and helped her to her feet. To my surprise, she started laughing. Before you knew it, we were the best of friends, inseparable. And years later, she even married my younger brother.

"Lesson to you, my dear daughter, always watch where you are going." Momma finished her story with a smile and dumped the potatoes into the pot of boiling water.

I just love listening to Momma tell stories. Her words are a mixture of Swedish and American, and she always has something interesting to say. How I love her.

June 24, 1854

Dear Diary,

Farren and Kirsten came over after school, and we hung out in our barn loft. Bethy and Laura came up too, and we all had fun playing together. Jesse says that we are too old to be playing like children, but Momma always says, "Your imagination is a creative tool, used to help you grow and learn." That quieted Jesse's teasing for the day!

June 26, 1854

Dear Diary,

Momma, Jesse, and I rode into town today. Our first stop was the general store. Momma had groceries to pick up, and she needed some cotton for a shirt for Poppa. She also

9

picked up some thread and said in a teasing tone to Jesse and me, "Now don't fly off with it!" I laughed and Jesse threw me a confused look. I told him I would explain it later.

Our next stop was the post office. Unfortunately, there were no letters from Sweden, but there was a letter from Poppa's brother, Uncle Philip, who lives in Missouri. Momma mailed three letters--one to *Mormor*, one to *Farmor*, and one to Aunt Melissa.

Last on our list was the blacksmith shop. Poppa needed us to pick up some nails and a new hammer head. Then we headed home.

June 27, 1854

Dear Diary,

Today is Sunday again. I just can't believe how fast the weeks fly by! Reverend Mast preached on patience and how we must all be patient toward one another. I always leave his service's feeling inspired, but I often find it hard to act on it the rest of the week. When I mentioned this to Poppa, he told me that I must constantly pray about it and try really hard to do just that.

June 30, 1854

Dear Diary,

School was pretty sorrowful today. Farren is sick with cholera. I could hardly believe it when I found out the news. I mean, I just saw her at church and now she is dreadfully sick. As soon as Bethy, Laura, and I got home, I told Momma about it. She turned quite pale and said that we would not be going to school anymore. Laura jumped up and down with excitement, but Bethy and I were thoroughly disappointed. I wanted to ride over to Kirsten's house to see if Aunt Maria was having her stay home too, but Momma quickly said, "No, Carolyn. It's best to stay put. Cholera's a dangerous sickness; not one to mess around with." I said nothing more on the subject and helped Momma make supper.

July 1, 1854

Dear Diary,

Even though we didn't go to school today, Momma sat us girls down and had us do our schoolwork anyways. Poor Laura! She had thought that she could play outside all day long. Our little Laura would live outside if she could.

When our school lessons were done for the morning, I

went out to the loft to work on my book. I would've worked on it upstairs, but Momma would've questioned what I was doing and I didn't want to lie or ruin the surprise. Right now, I'm at the part when Momma and Poppa are telling our extended family of our leaving. It is really quite sad. If I close my eyes, I can still see *Mormor's* face when we told her the news--ashen white, tears welling in her questioning eyes. Just thinking about her makes me want to cry. I miss her so much. I know grandmothers shouldn't have favorites, but I think I am her favorite granddaughter, and she was my favorite *Mormor.* How I long to see her again!

July 2, 1854

Dear Diary,

Momma and I made a raspberry pie this afternoon. And of course, I was granted a story. This one was about Momma's first pie making experience:

"Now, let's see, I believe I was about your age or a little younger when I was going to make my very first pie by myself. Momma was out for the afternoon with one of her friends and I had decided that I would surprise her with a pie for dessert tonight. Well, I began trying to remember

Momma's recipe as best I could, for of course, she kept it in her head. Finally, it was in the oven and I was very proud of myself. So, I decided to head outside and read for a little bit. I must've gotten engrossed in my book, for my older brother Kaleb came running out of the house yelling fire. I ran inside, but there was no fire, just billows of smoke pouring from the stove. Quickly, I pulled my pie from the oven. It was burnt, but nothing a little whipped topping couldn't fix. After making Kaleb promise not to tell, I cleaned the house of smoke as well as I could and made a whipped topping for my pie.

"Supper came and went, and soon it was time for dessert. I pulled out my pie and served everyone a big, heaping spoonful. Kaleb's face was priceless. He did not want to eat it after he saw what happened to it. Levi took a big bite. Suddenly, his face got all red, and he started choking. As I looked around, Momma and Poppa looked the same as Levi. Apparently, my pie was burnt, and I had also misplaced the sugar with the salt.

"Momma told me, 'Juliana, next time, get the recipe from me and never leave the house while baking.' I have never forgotten her words. And you better not either!" We both burst into laughter. I can almost imagine the looks on

Uncle Kaleb, Uncle Levi, Grandpa, and *Mormor's* faces. That would have been a sight to see!

July 4, 1854

Dear Diary,

Poppa and Momma thought it best if we didn't go to Sunday services. With all the sickness floating around, they wanted to stay isolated. So after a little service of our own, I went up to the loft to write more of my story. I just wrote the part about boarding the ship. I can still remember the feeling of standing aboard that ship and looking out at all my family waving good-bye on the dock. Kirsten and I clasped hands as the ship pulled away, leaving the figures of so many beloved ones getting tinier and tinier. Poppa put his strong hand on my shoulder and looked down at me, eyes shining with love. "Things will get better, my Carrie. America has many opportunities to offer us." I believed him then, and I still do. As I'm looking back, I realize that I trusted him with everything, just as Reverend Mast had said we need to trust God with everything.

July 6, 1854

Dear Diary,

Poppa just found out that many more families have been inflicted with cholera. Seven are from our school. I can hardly believe that this is happening. Sickness is a dreadful thing. When I asked Poppa what exactly cholera is, he told me that it comes from contaminated water. "Then why must we stay away from those who are sick?" Poppa sighed. "It's complicated, Carrie. It's best just to keep distance to be on the safe side."

July 7, 1854

Dear Diary,

Today, I longed so much to see Kirsten and Farren that I rode Lucia over to Kirsten's house. At the time I was so consumed with wanting to see them that I didn't even think of the consequences.

Once I got to Kirsten's house, we agreed that we would ride over to Farren's house, just to see if she was possibly better. Her younger brother was outside and said that Farren wasn't better at all. We were very disappointed. When I got home, I was so distraught at hearing the news about Farren that I broke down and told Momma.

With disappointment in her eyes she said, "Oh, Carolyn, how could you?"

"I just had to see her, Momma. I'm sorry." But I could tell Momma was still very disappointed in me. She told Poppa and they decided that I had to weed the garden (my least favorite chore). Well, I learned my lesson. Never disobey Momma and Poppa again. I think the hurt showing on their faces was punishment enough for me.

July 8, 1854

Dear Diary,

As you well know, I have been weeding the garden most of the morning. We have a rather large garden--peas, beans, carrots, onions, potatoes, beets, and corn. It was a back-breaking task.

The afternoon was much more pleasant. I wrote some more in my book. This part was about our time on the ship. Momma, Bethy, and I were all seasick pretty much the entire two weeks we were on the ship. It was such a rocky experience; I hope I never have to go on a boat again!

July 9, 1854

Dear Diary,

Momma, Bethy, and I did some sewing this afternoon.
I don't really enjoy sewing, but it is better than weeding.
Momma told a story to us while we worked. This one was
about when Momma made her first patchwork quilt. Bethy
and I wanted to see it so badly after Momma had finished her
story, but Momma said that she must've left it in Sweden. As
she said that, her eyes had a faraway look in them as if
remembering life back in Sweden.

July 11, 1854

Dear Diary,

I can hardly believe that it has been almost two weeks
since this cholera started. It is now another Sunday that we
have not gone to services. Poppa read to us from 1 Peter 1:21.
It says, *"Through Christ you have come to trust in God. And you
have placed your faith and hope in God because He raised Christ
from the dead and gave Him great glory."* Sometimes I still
marvel that Christ really died to save me and now He is risen
from the dead and living in glory. Such a marvelous thing to
have happened!

July 13, 1854

Dear Diary,

Farren has died from cholera. This news is so shocking to me that my mind can hardly make sense of it. It seems like just yesterday we were playing together and now we never will again.

July 14, 1845

Dear Diary,

I cried myself to sleep last night. It was dreadful. Later this morning, Momma showed me a verse in Matthew that helped calm my spirits. *"Blessed are those who mourn, for they shall be comforted."* (Matthew 5:4). God will make everything right in the end and someday I will get to see Farren again.

July 16, 1854

Dear Diary,

Cholera is now spreading to those I love. Momma and I were in the kitchen making bread when we heard a pounding at the door. Luke was very much out of breath. He didn't come in, but only said, "Its Herb and Kirsten. They're sick with the cholera." I covered my mouth with my hands.

My dear Kirsten...I don't think I could bear it if she died also. Momma said that she would go over, but Luke replied that he was only supposed to tell us the news. Uncle Levi had said that they will be all right. Momma seemed to accept this news reluctantly. "Very well. But come get me if things get worse." Luke nodded, then he was off. I still can't believe this is really happening.

July 17, 1854

Dear Diary,

    This morning, Momma had Laura and I go weed the garden. The chore is not half as bad when you have a companion! Laura was very chatty. Suddenly, she leaned her head into me and closed her eyes. I felt her forehead, and she was burning up with a fever. Quickly, I brought her inside to Momma, who scooped Laura up and carried her upstairs. On her way up, she yelled to me bring some water and cool cloths. I quickly did so and then she told me to tell Poppa.

    Running outside, I looked all around for Poppa, but I couldn't find him anywhere. Finally, I caught sight of him walking back toward the house with Jesse. "Poppa, Poppa!" My cries of alarm stopped him midway and I ran to him.

"Laura's sick." Those were the only words that I needed to say. Poppa dashed to the house.

Jesse and I followed Poppa inside and found Bethy sitting in the living room. She looked up when we came in and asked, "She will be okay, right, Carolyn?" I sat down next to her and wrapped my arms around her. "Of course she will, Bethy. We all will." I can only hope I spoke the truth.

July 18, 1854

Dear Diary,

Momma woke me up bright and early this morning. "Come, Carolyn," she whispered. "Poppa's sick. We have much work to do."

I dressed quickly and hurried downstairs to begin a long, hard day of work. Momma had me first make breakfast for Jesse, Bethy, and myself; then I was to put on a pot of chicken broth and a pot of hot water. "Everything they touch must be boiled," she told me very sternly. And that was my job.

Around noon, Jesse and Bethy went out to feed the animals. I took some broth and water up to the sickroom for Momma. Momma had moved Laura out of our loft and to her

bedroom so we would have less running around to do. When
I went in the room, I didn't see Momma, so I set my dishes
down and walked over to the bed. Poppa and Laura were
both flushed and when I felt Laura, she was burning up. I
took a cool cloth and placed it on her forehead. Then I
rounded the bed to do the same for Poppa. On the floor next
to the bed, I found Momma! I knelt down beside her and she
was burning up just like Poppa and Laura. Not sure what I
should do, I flew outside to get Jesse.

He came inside and I made a pallet for Momma on the
floor at the end of the bed. Together, we half carried, half
dragged her onto it. When we got Momma situated, I told
Jesse to go and tell Bethy to keep an eye on the water and
bring me some more cloths and drinking water. I held my
hand against Momma's beloved face. How could she get sick?
What was I to do? How could I care for them all?

Bethy came in with what I asked for. I tried to prop
Momma up and give her a drink, but when she wouldn't take
it, I laid her back down and put wet cloths on her head. We
went to the kitchen and I showed Bethy what to do. I gave her
a quick hug and then went back to my patients. It was going
to be a long night.

July 19, 1854

Dear Diary,

Today has been such a long day. Bethy and I have
been taking turns in the kitchen and in the sickroom. It is such
tiring work. Whenever we give someone a drink or a
spoonful of broth, we then have to go and wash it in boiling
water. Feeding is not an easy task either. Bethy and I try to do
it together whenever possible, for one of us holds them up
and the other feeds. I rely so heavily on my sister, but I don't
want to wear her out and make her susceptible too.

Jesse stays outside most of the day, unless I need his
help with something. He only comes in for meals (which
aren't elaborate) and to bring in handfuls of wood to keep our
fire hot. I asked him to go for the doctor, but he said his
search would be futile because he wouldn't know where the
doctor would be. I can only pray that Doc. Martin will check
up on us.

July 20, 1854

Dear Diary,

I am so afraid. Little Laura is burning up. She'll be
shivering cold one minute and so I'll cover her with blankets,

and then she will be sweating up a storm. She tosses and turns and her fever is very high. Poppa is pretty bad too, as is Momma, though she isn't as bad yet.

Jesse had to go out to the woods to cut some more firewood and so I sent Bethy with him. It will be good for her to get some fresh air and a break. Without her here, I confined myself in the kitchen, watching the pots.

July 21, 1854

Dear Diary,

These days are so long, but I managed to convince Jesse and Bethy to sleep. I try to sleep as well, but my mind always seems to wander and I find myself thinking about every bad thing that could possibly happen.

Last night, I was so distraught over everything that was happening that I finally opened my Bible. I opened it to James. James 5:14-15 says, "*Is anyone among you sick? Let him call for the elders of the church, and let them pray over him, anointing him with oil in the name of the Lord. And the prayer of faith will save the one who is sick, and the Lord will raise him up.*" After reading that, I felt so encouraged that I prayed for Momma, Poppa, Laura, Kirsten, Herb, and anyone else who was sick that they might be healed. Then I also prayed for

Jesse, Bethy, and I to stay well so that we would be able to take care of those around us. I felt much better after that.

July 22, 1854

Dear Diary,

Nothing is changing, but I keep reminding myself to trust God and He will take care of us. I sent Jesse to Aunt Maria's to see if she knew where the doctor was. He didn't want to go, but I told him we would manage fine. What we need right now is a doctor----some help. I don't know what else to do for Momma, Poppa, and Laura then what I am doing right now.

July 23, 1854

Dear Diary,

As I was stirring the broth, a thought came to me. Perhaps mint tea would be helpful for my patients. Of course, we had none in our herb supply, so Bethy went out to get some. Meanwhile, Jesse has not returned, and I can only guess that he is going from farmhouse to farmhouse, hoping to find the doctor.

Momma, Poppa, and Laura show no improvement. In

fact, they seem to be getting worse. When Bethy returned, we made some warm mint tea, but they're not drinking it too well. I will keep trying though.

July 24, 1854

Dear Diary,

Poppa seems to be doing a little better; not quite so feverish. Momma and Laura are still pretty bad. Bethy is getting pretty pale, but whenever I check her for a fever, there is none. I try to make her lie down, but I need her help. I wouldn't be able to do this without her.

There has been no word on Jesse. I'm beginning to fear that he is sick and not able to find us. How far away could he be? The only thing I can do is trust him to God, but sometimes even that doesn't send my worries away.

July 25, 1854

Dear Diary,

This morning, Bethy tended to Momma, Poppa, and Laura, changing their cloths and trying to give them some water. I was in the kitchen, trying to make a mint spread to put on their chests. I'm not exactly sure what I was trying to

accomplish, but it
wouldn't hurt to try.

While I was in
the kitchen, there was
a knock on the door.
It surprised me, for
there have been no
visitors at our place
since Luke dropped
by that dreadful day.
Before I opened the
door, I yelled out that

there was cholera in the house. The man replied back, "Yes,
ma'am, I know. But I think I have your brother with me." I
flung open the door and there in the man's arms was Jesse. I
felt his face and it was burning up. I looked up at the man.
"Thank you for bringing him back. He was looking for the
doctor. My parents are sick too." The man looked back at me
with sorrowful eyes. "I wish I could help, miss, but I really
must be going." He placed Jesse in my arms and raced out of
the yard. I almost collapsed from the weight of my brother.
"Bethy! Come outside!" Bethy was out instantly and we
carried Jesse, or tried to, into the sickroom and on the floor

near Momma's makeshift bed.

Bethy went to the kitchen to get some water and I applied cloths to his head. He opened his eyes one at a time and whispered, "I didn't find the doctor, Carrie. I'm sorry." I put my cool hand on the side of his burning face. "Don't worry, Jesse. It will be okay." I closed my eyes to hold the tears at bay. What were we going to do? How could Bethy and I manage alone?

July 26, 1854

Dear Diary,

As relieved as I am to have Jesse back home with us, it is hard work taking care of one more person on top of Momma, Poppa, and Laura. Not to mention worrying about him too. Somehow, Bethy and I are managing. Every morning, she goes out to feed the animals, while I get another pot of broth on and find something for our breakfast. Then, we go and reapply the cloths to their heads. Just today, we started putting my mint salve on their chests and foreheads. I'm hoping that the minty smell will soothe their unsettled stomachs. After that process is done, Bethy goes to stir the broth and I get fresh water cups and we try to get them to drink a little. Lunchtime, we try to find something to eat. After lunch, I went outside to get some wood to add to our fire and then we go feed our patients some broth. Most of the time, they won't take any, but we try anyway. The days seem to last forever. I am lucky if I catch a few hours of sleep before I hear someone cough and have to run to make sure they are okay.

Right now, Momma is the worst off of the four of them. I'm dreadfully worried about her and I hope the doctor gets here soon.

July 27, 1854

Dear Diary,

Poppa is better! I can hardly believe it, but he really, truly is! His fever broke sometime this morning. Bethy and I moved him to the living room (believe me, it was hard work!). He lost so much weight because of not eating much, but now we were about to get some good broth into him. Now I just have to continue to put good nourishment in him and get Momma, Laura, and Jesse better.

July 28, 1854

Dear Diary,

Since Poppa is out in the other room, Bethy and I moved Momma up on the bed and off the floor. As I was changing the cloths on her head, she opened her eyes and whispered in a hoarse voice, "Where's your Poppa, Carolyn?"

"Don't worry, Momma. Poppa's better. He's downstairs."

Momma gave a faint smile. "Good." She closed her eyes again and seemed to go back asleep. I was pleased to have a little conversation with Momma. Perhaps it means she is on the mend.

July 29, 1854

Dear Diary,

Luke rode over while I was outside getting wood. I must have looked a fright, because the first thing he asked was, "Are you feeling okay, Carolyn?"

I readjusted the wood in my arms, "As well as can be expected."

He slid down from his horse and took the wood from my arms. "Herb died last night."

I stared at him, "What? I'm so sorry."

He walked with me to the house and dropped the wood in the wood box. "Momma's devastated, but with Kirsten and Poppa still sick, there's not much she can do."

I gave him a sad smile. "Thanks for coming to tell me." He left then, leaving me with an empty feeling. First Farren, and now my eldest cousin died from this awful cholera.

I told Poppa and Bethy the news. My little sister had tears in her eyes and Poppa suggested that we all pray for Uncle Levi, Aunt Maria, Luke, and Kirsten. So we did.

July 30, 1854

Dear Diary,

My mint salve doesn't seem to help Momma, Laura, or Jesse. So I decided to experiment a bit in the kitchen. I tried adding some other herbs in with it and even put some garlic in. Once I had finished, I took it to the sick room, and Bethy and I applied it to their chests and foreheads.

As I was putting it on Jesse, he opened his eyes and said, "Really, Carrie? Garlic?"

I smiled at him and continued rubbing. "You better get used to it. It might make you better."

At the end of the day, I'm not sure if it made any difference or not, but it didn't hurt to try.

July 31, 1854

Dear Diary,

Not much has happened. Momma and Jesse are still pretty bad. Laura seems to be getting a little better, but she is still feverish. It is hard to watch my baby sister toss and turn from this sickness that is taking over her body.

August 1, 1854

Dear Diary,

Where is the doctor? I can't believe that we have not seen him at all. You would think that he would be making regular rounds to check on his patients.

We have run out of wood, so I went out to chop some. I could not believe that I was actually out chopping wood, in August no less! I had never before lifted an ax!

As I was chopping, Cole Brown came walking by. He gave a low, mean sort of whistle. "Well, well, what have we here? Little Miss Carolyn chopping wood. Can't your big brother do it for you?"

I whirled around; ax in hand. "My whole family, except Bethany, is sick. If you were any kind of gentleman, you would offer to cut this for me." He laughed and instead of taking my ax, shoved my pile of chopped wood so that it rolled all over. Then he walked away, laughing at me. I continued chopping and then leaned down and picked up my pieces and brought them back to the house. It still puzzles me at how some people can be so mean.

August 2, 1854

Dear Diary,

Luke came by today and informed us that Doc. Martin was dead. I could hardly believe it. "What?"

Luke shrugged. "I know. They sent for a new doctor, but who knows when he will get here."

I can't believe this is happening. I hope he gets here soon, before anything tragic happens to my family.

August 3, 1854

Dear Diary,

My day started out as normal. Bethy and I had changed the cloths and mint/garlic salve, and now she was in the kitchen starting the broth and I in the sick room trying to see if Momma would drink anything. I had just laid her back down, when she clasped my hand. In a very soft, croaky voice, she murmured, "Carolyn, take care of the housework. Mind your Poppa and brother, and take care of your sisters. Teach them all that I have taught you. And don't forget..." she paused, took a shaky breath, and continued, "Don't forget all that I have taught you. I love..." She didn't finish.

"Momma?" I touched the side of her face, but she was gone. Tears sprang in my eyes. What would I do without Momma? I covered her beloved face and went to tell Poppa and Bethy.

Bethy screamed when I told her and she ran outside. Poppa was crying too, but he still pulled me in his arms and held me close. I cried against Poppa for the longest time. Poppa kissed my forehead, then whispered, "We will be alright, my Carrie. God will help us." For once, I didn't believe that God would truly help us. If He wanted to, He should've left Momma here. But she was gone. Gone from our life forever.

August 4, 1854

Dear Diary,

Bethy went to Uncle Levi's this morning to tell them the news about Momma. I can tell that Poppa is grieving, because he was out in the barn the whole day. I managed to convince him not to chop wood. He didn't have enough strength for that yet. With Momma gone, I moved Jesse up into Momma's place on the bed, after I had changed the sheets. I was determined not to fail with Jesse and Laura. I had to make them better, but I was running out of ideas.

In every barn of every household, someone had placed caskets. We placed Momma in ours and Poppa dug a grave. He and Bethy held a little service for Momma, but I stayed inside with Jesse and Laura. Her grave is near the barn, not in eyesight from the house, but close enough to go to. I'm not sure I'm quite ready to visit Momma at her grave.

August 5, 1854

Dear Diary,

I have such a feeling of guilt welling inside of me. I feel that Momma's death is my fault. If only I had done something different. As I was sitting down next to Poppa while he was eating, he asked me if something was wrong. I wasn't planning on telling anyone how I felt, but it just sort of came out.

He put his soup bowl down and pulled me into a hug. "Oh Carolyn, Momma's death is not your fault. God wanted her with him, and there was nothing you or I could've done about it."

I started crying again. "But I should've tried harder."

Poppa covered my head with his large hand. "You did, my Carrie, you did the best that you have done. You did everything you could have done. The rest was in God's hands." The tears continued to fall, but Poppa's words made me feel somewhat better.

August 6, 1854

Dear Diary,

Laura seems like she's getting better. I heard word that the new doctor has arrived and is making his way around our community. I don't quite understand why they didn't send more than one doctor. Jesse and Laura don't know yet that Momma has passed. I'm hoping they don't find out that she is gone before they are well enough to take the news.

August 7, 1854

Dear Diary,

Dr. Richards has arrived! We are thrilled! He checked Laura and said that she was indeed over the worst, but he wasn't quite sure about Jesse yet. He said that I did a good job getting nourishment back into Poppa. Then he left. I wasn't quite sure what I thought the doctor would do, but I thought he would do more than this. Dr. Richards didn't tell me anything that I didn't already know.

August 8, 1854

Dear Diary,

Laura is better; her fever broke late last night. When

she awoke, she asked for Momma. I told her that Momma
was with Jesus now and she cried and cried. I held her in my
arms until she fell asleep. Thank God that I didn't lose my
baby sister. Her little heart must have broken in two when I
told her about her beloved mother. I know mine did.

August 9, 1854

Dear Diary,

We brought Laura downstairs and fed her some
chicken broth today. I am relieved to see her sitting up and
slowly eating. I know she is anxious to get outside again.
Jesse is still doing pretty poorly. Poppa is able to help Bethy
with the chores now, so that will relieve her of some stress.
My days are still as busy as they always were. I almost went
out to Momma's grave today, but then I just couldn't bring
myself to do it.

August 10, 1854

Dear Diary,

Jesse's fever broke this morning. I was applying some
of my garlic/mint salve, when his eyes flickered open. I
almost screamed with delight but instead reached down and

gave him a hug. He gave a soft chuckle. "Well, someone is certainly glad to see me awake."

I laughed, while my eyes filled with tears of joy. "You are the last to get well."

Jesse smiled. "Good. Can you get this awful stuff off of me now?"

Instead of removing it, I ran out into the living room to let the rest of my family know. "Jesse's well!" My voice rang through the house. Bethy met me mid-run and we embraced. It is a lovely feeling to know that my family is well again. A cold realization came over me. Momma wasn't here. She never would be again. Somehow, I would have to tell Jesse the news. I went back in his room, but he had fallen asleep. "Tomorrow," I whispered softly, tucking more covers around his pale body. "Tomorrow I'll tell you about Momma."

August 11, 1854

Dear Diary,

Even though my mind rested easier knowing that Jesse was well, I still didn't sleep that great. I am still consumed with thoughts of Momma's death, and I feel as though my heart is broken. I brought Jesse up some chicken broth and while he was eating, I told him the news.

He didn't cry, though I'm not sure if I was expecting him to or not. "It would've helped if I had found the doctor." He was struggling with guilt like I had, or do.

I placed my hand on his arm, "It's not your fault. A couple days after you were returned, Luke came by and told me that Doc. Martin was dead. Then, once Dr. Richards, came, he didn't give me anything that would've made a difference."

He looked down at his soup. "I guess you're right. How did I get here anyway?"

I gave a small smile, and then told him the whole story. "I think it was an angel. I didn't recognize him, and he didn't tell me his name or stay to help." A sudden realization came to me. "God was with us the whole time, even when He took Momma away." The tears came again, and Jesse grasped my hand and squeezed it reassuringly. I never before felt this bond with my brother. Sickness and death must pull a family together more than I realized.

August 12, 1854

Dear Diary,

I decided to go ride over to Aunt Maria's today and see how they were all doing and tell all that has happened here. After leaving Bethy with instructions on how to look after Jesse and Laura (she probably knew them all, but I suppose it was my "maternal" instinct), I left.

Luke and Uncle Levi were both outside when I arrived. Seeing Uncle Levi, I was reminded of how much he looked like Momma. I slid off my horse and ran into his arms, sobbing. I'm sure he was very weak yet from just recovering, but that didn't stop him from comforting me. It seems as if I've been crying every day since Momma passed.

Aunt Maria must have heard the noise. She came out of the house and enveloped me in a hug as well. When I had finished crying, I looked up and dried my eyes. "Sorry."

Aunt Maria grasped my shoulders. "Oh, my darling child, don't you ever apologize. You have every right to cry after what you have been through."

I gave her a sad smile. "So do you."

She looked at me with a sad face, and then said, more cheerfully, "Kirsten's inside. She wanted to come out and see you so bad, but I insisted that she stay put and I would send you in."

My smile was genuine this time, and I ran inside and embraced my best friend. It was wonderful to sit and talk with her after almost a month of not talking. I told her everything that had happened since we last saw each other. Before long, it was time for me to go. I didn't want to have Bethy make supper in addition to taking care of Jesse and Laura.

I gave Kirsten one last hug. "I'll come again."

She smiled at me. "Good. Then we can talk some more." I knew she was referring to Momma, but I just smiled and left. I didn't want to get into that right now.

August 13, 1854

Dear Diary,

Things are slowly going back to normal. Poppa is doing more and more of the outside work, Laura is keeping down more solid foods, and Jesse is drinking lots of broth. He is getting pretty tired of it, I think. Poppa still isn't strong enough to chop wood, so I went out. I don't think he liked it very much. "Oh, please, Poppa, I did it before, and I can do it again." He didn't argue with me, partly because I think he knew he couldn't do it. Lucky for me, I didn't meet up with anyone else in my chopping experience. I had almost forgotten how tiring this work really was. I am desperately hoping that Poppa regains his strength by the next time we need more wood.

August 14, 1854

Dear Diary,

I decided to do some cleaning today. Now that everyone is well, or almost, we need to get this awful cholera out of here. Ever since Poppa put a well in our yard, we don't have to go to the lake to gather water for washing, which is really nice.

At the end of the day, after the house had been cleaned and everyone has eaten a good meal, I finally collapsed and rested. I'm hoping that in the next couple days I can start working on my book again. Though now Momma won't be here to read it. Just the thought made me start crying again. I wish I could stop crying with every thought of Momma.

August 15, 1854

Dear Dairy,

I had an awful dream last night. I was in the kitchen washing up the dishes, when Momma's voice called, "Carolyn, come, I need some help." I searched the whole house looking for her and then I came back to the kitchen, and she was lying on the floor, dead. I woke up crying. I'm surprised I didn't scream. What am I going to do without her? How will I survive?

August 17, 1854

Dear Diary,

We received word this morning saying that school was opening up again tomorrow. I'm going to send Bethy and Laura, but after talking it over with Poppa, he agreed that I could stay home. I'm glad, even though I love school. It will be good to devote my time to doing the job that Momma wanted me to do--take care of her house.

August 18, 1854

Dear Diary,

After Bethy and Laura left for school, Poppa and Jesse

went outside to check on our corn crop. I stood in the house alone. I could hear every little noise, even the birds outside. I don't know how Momma did this every day. It's a lonely sort of feeling. I don't even know what she did during the day because I was at school. "I need your help, Momma. I don't know what to do." I voiced my thoughts aloud, not exactly speaking to anyone in particular. "I suppose I need you too, God. Please help me. I don't know how to be a housekeeper or mother." Momma wanted me to teach Bethy and Laura everything that she had taught me. How was I to do that? Momma had years of wisdom, and I was still learning.

By the time Poppa and Jesse came home for lunch, I had a chicken roasting for supper, the bread had just come out of the oven, and the garden was weeded. Later that afternoon, I decided to do some mending. Before cholera came, Momma was planning on making Poppa a new shirt, so that is what I decided to do. And now I have to figure out what to do tomorrow.

August 19, 1854

Dear Diary,

I decided that sooner or a later I would have to go

through Momma's trunk. Well, I suppose I didn't have to, but
I needed some sewing needles for my mending after I broke
the two that I have, and Momma keeps her sewing kit in her
trunk.

Slowly, I knelt down in front of her trunk. I had never
been through Momma's possessions. She had told me once
that her trunk contained many of the memories from Sweden.
Taking a deep breath, I opened the trunk. Momma's scent
flooded over me and I almost had to forgo my mission
because I was so overwhelmed. Instead, I reached my hand in
and pulled out Momma's sewing kit. I had found what I was
looking for. I could leave, but curiosity begged me to stay.
Looking in, I pulled out two white candlesticks--St. Lucia
candles that we use every year around Christmas. Next I
pulled out an old photograph of our family right before we
left Sweden and another one of Momma and Poppa's
wedding. Next, a beautiful quilt came out and I knew it was
from *Mormor* when we left Sweden. In the folds of the quilt,
there was an old book. Momma's diary. I couldn't believe it.
Inside, were stories, stories that Momma had told me and
many more. I couldn't wait to beginning reading. I was
getting ready to put all of her things back in the trunk, when I
came across a doll lying on the bottom. I reached in and

picked it up. It was Momma's rag doll. I took the rag doll, diary, and sewing kit with me and placed everything else back in the trunk. Now I'm glad I went through Momma's trunk.

August 20, 1854

Dear Diary,

As I was baking today, I was remembering back to the days before the cholera came. How happy we were. I remember my birthday and my excitement when Momma handed me my diary and told me, "Carolyn, you are now old enough to be keeping a diary of your own. You may put anything and everything in it. Only your eyes, and that of God's, will see what you write."

Suddenly, I came to the realization that we had missed Laura's birthday. I racked my brain, trying to remember the day. It was August 3rd--the day Momma died. I hurried out to the barn to tell Poppa. He told me that we must have a celebration. We decided on Monday evening.

August 21, 1854

Dear Diary,

We went to church today. How glad I was to be back among my friends again, though I could tell many were missing. Reverend Mast preached on putting our hope in God. Psalm 18:4-6 says, *"The ropes of death entangled me; floods of destruction swept over me. The grave wrapped its ropes around me; death laid a trap in my path. But in my distress I cried out to the Lord; yes, I prayed to my God for help."* That verse spoke to me. Death is all around us, but God is still with us. I prayed for him to heal Poppa, Jesse, and Laura. I prayed for his help in running the household like Momma did. God answered those prayers, even if he didn't answer my prayer concerning Momma. Reverend Mast was saying that we need to trust God no matter what; when he answers our prayers and when he doesn't. God's timing is perfect.

August 22, 1854

Dear Diary,

While Bethy and Laura were in school, I cooked and baked for this evening's party. In addition to my cooking, I also cleaned the house. When the girls got home, they set the table while I did last minute baking. Around suppertime, Poppa and Jesse came inside and Aunt Maria, Uncle Levi, Luke, and Kirsten arrived. It was a glorious time, and everyone was happy in the midst of our sorrow.

Laura received a surprising number of gifts, even though the party was so last minute. Poppa and Jesse had made Laura a little wooden horse and sleigh; Bethy gave her a new apron; Kirsten and Aunt Maria made a new shawl; Uncle Levi and Luke made clay dishes for her doll; and I gave her a present from Momma. "Laura, while I was looking upstairs in Momma's trunk a couple days ago, I came across something that I really think she would like you to have." I handed my gift to her, and she opened it and screamed. It was Momma's rag doll that I had fixed up a bit. Laura gave me a big hug. Even though she has another doll, I know this one will be special because it was Momma's.

August 23, 1854

Dear Diary,

Today, I longed to go to school, but instead, I stayed home and did the wash and mended. I wish I could've sat down and wrote in my book. I wish I could be with my friends. I wish I could go on a horseback ride. I wish Momma were here. It seems as though I am longing for everything I don't have. If Momma were here, she would've said, "Carolyn, don't complain. Be thankful for what you have."

August 24, 1854

Dear Diary,

When I was baking today, I started talking to Momma. I asked her, "Momma, did you ever wish that you were someone else?" I imagined her answer would be, "Carolyn, you can imagine you're someone else, but you can't and won't be someone else. You'll always be my Carolyn." Her answers always bring me comfort, because I can almost imagine that I really am hearing her voice. Sometimes I wish I could be someone else, but then, I wouldn't have learned all that I have learned from Momma and Poppa. I wouldn't have Jesse, Bethy, or Laura. I wouldn't have any of my family. God knew what he was doing when he made me a Woodsmall.

August 25, 1854

Dear Diary,

I decided to go on a ride on Lucia this morning. It was

so peaceful and calming. I felt a sense of almost pure joy. When I got back, I was reading my bible when I came across Psalm 19:1, *"The heavens declare the glory of God, and the sky above proclaims his handiwork."* As I was out on my ride, I could see God's handiwork all around: the sky and the perfect cloud formations, the trees, the birds, and all the animals. Everything around me was declaring God's glory. I am so glad that I have a God who is almighty and still takes care of little me. He created everything, and yet he protects me.

August 26, 1854

Dear Diary,

Hannah Miller stopped by today. They don't live that far away from us, and she said she was driving home and decided to stop in and see how I was doing. I told her that we were doing pretty well, and I offered her a piece of pie. She told me, "You are turning into a lovely housewife, Carolyn. Your mother would be mighty proud of you."

Mrs. Miller lost her husband in a fire last year, so she knows the pain of losing someone you love. She has two boys; Henry, who is twelve, and Jake, who is nine.

Before she left, I invited her and her boys over for

supper on September 3rd. I could tell that she was pleased with my invitation. I hope I know what I got myself into. I've never done a supper for someone besides family without Momma.

August 27, 1854

Dear Diary,

Being that today was a Saturday, Poppa took us all into town. He needed to pick up some lumber and I had some items I needed at the general store. When we arrived, Poppa dropped Bethy, Laura, and I off. It seemed strange to be shopping without Momma. We received many sympathetic faces from those who knew about Momma. I picked out the things I needed, and then paid Mrs. Holly for my purchases. Holding my basket in one hand, I grasped Laura's hand and we walked across the street to the lumber mill where Poppa and Jesse were waiting for us.

August 28, 1854

Dear Diary,

We had church services today. Reverend Mast read to us from Romans 15:4. It says, *"Such things were written in the*

Scriptures long ago to teach us. And the Scriptures give us hope and encouragement as we wait patiently for God's promises to be fulfilled." God is always with us and he will always keep his promises. When I read about God's promises, I am filled with hope. Sometimes it seems as though all hope has vanished from my life. But in his Word, God promises that he has a plan for my life and I can have hope. I just need to trust him with everything.

August 29, 1854

Dear Diary,

It rained today, so I took that as the perfect excuse to work on my book. I just got to the part of our arrival in America. When we arrived at Ellis Island, Momma was so seasick they kept her on the island in the sick area. We were so afraid she would be taken back to Sweden, but she was soon better and it was determined that she was only seasick. It was a very joyful day when Momma came back through the port and we were reunited with her.

When the girls got home from school, Laura bounced in with a look of sheer happiness, while Bethy wore a look of sadness. "School is finished!" Laura said, as she placed her wet things where I showed her to. I smiled, "Only for a month or so." Laura glared at me, but I earned a smile from Bethy. I'm sort of happy my sisters are home. Now I can have some company.

August 30, 1854

Dear Diary,

Bethy, Laura, and I headed into the woods today to pick some raspberries. While we were out there, we stayed in a close vicinity of each other, and I told them a story. It was about the time when Momma was a young girl picking raspberries in Sweden. Unfortunately, she ate too many and that night she had a terrible stomach ache. "*Mormor* had told Momma, 'Juliana, I hoped you learn your lesson. Do what you have been told. If you would have done what I had asked and picked the berries, you would not be writhing in pain and would've had dessert.'"

Laura laughed at my impersonation of *Mormor's* voice, but Bethy had tears in her eyes. "Whatever is the matter, Bethy?" I asked her, concerned at what could be wrong with my story.

She wiped her tears away and tried to smile. "You

53

sounded just like Momma when you told us a story with a lesson to it." Joy and sadness welled up inside of me: joy, because I was teaching them as Momma asked, and sadness, because Momma wasn't.

August 31, 1854

Dear Diary,

The girls and I survived a long, hot day in the kitchen. Of course the one day we decided to can, it decides to be very hot and sticky. Laura washed all the berries, Bethy mashed and stirred them in a hot pot, and I loaded them into jars. A very long process considering the amount of berries we picked yesterday. We were in the kitchen till past lunch, though we did take a break to eat and feed Poppa and Jesse. Then we worked part of the afternoon, cleaned up, and had to get started on supper. How relieved was I to finally sit down and sew!

September 1, 1854

Dear Diary,

Time to harvest our garden. Laura, Bethy, and I picked peas, beans, and red beets; pulled carrots; and dug potatoes. Then Laura washed them, Bethy cut them, and I put them into jars and canned them. Even though this harvesting takes so much hard work, it is nice to see that we have plenty of food for this winter. I do wish Momma was here to help us though.

September 2, 1854

Dear Diary,

Still another busy day! While Laura and Jesse dug out the garden, Bethy and I cleaned the house from top to bottom. Since the Millers were coming over, I was determined to make a good impression on my first "company" meal without Momma.

September 3, 1854

Dear Diary,

Bethy and I baked the day away, and by the time we were done, we were very hot! By 6:30 in the evening, we had made pickled beets, green beans, potatoes, roasted carrots, peas, beef and gravy, fresh bread, strawberry pie, and raspberry pudding. When Poppa and Jesse walked in the house to change, they were clearly shocked by how much food we made. I don't know what they expected, but they both said that they couldn't wait to eat. When Mrs. Miller and her boys arrived at seven, we were ready. Everyone loved the meal and praised us for making it so delicious. At the end of the evening, Poppa told me later that he was very proud of the way I had handled myself.

September 4, 1854

Dear Diary,

After yesterday, I am exhausted, but we still had church services to attend. Reverend Mast read from Psalm 130:7, *"Hope in the Lord; for with the Lord there is unfailing love. His redemption overflows."* He talked about how God will love us no matter what we do, and he will always forgive us from our sins. All we have to do is go to him with a repentant heart.

Season 2

September 5, 1854

Dear Diary,

It seems as if the busyness will never cease. The harvest season is just beginning. For the harvest, we help our neighbors and friends by going over to their house when their corn, wheat, apples, or something else is ready to be picked. The men and boys work out in the fields, the ladies cook a meal, and the kids can play together. In the evening, there is a party of some sorts, more like a dance. Mr. Schafer brings out his fiddle, Mr. Caraff his banjo, and Mr. Moore his cello, and everyone dances till it is time to go back home.

Today we went to the Moore's house. I brought along some raspberry pudding for the meal (I forgot to mention that each family brings a food item). I helped in the kitchen mostly, but around mid-morning, Kirsten and I went out to bring water to the workers. It felt strange to be at the Moore's house without Farren being there. She always loved these times when everyone got together and made work fun.

We didn't stay too long for the dancing, because tomorrow the harvest is at Kirsten's and we are helping to set up.

September 6, 1854

Dear Diary,

Bright and early, we left for the Cradle farm. I brought homemade bread that I made late last night and a jar of red beets. When we got there, Uncle Levi and Luke were outside getting tables set up for the noonday meal, and Aunt Maria and Kirsten were bustling about inside. Soon other guests started arriving and I got so wrapped in my work that the time just flew by. All too soon, there was dancing and then we all had to go home.

I stayed up very late tonight and made some bread and pie crusts, for tomorrow the harvest is at our house. Oh my! I am very nervous to be doing this without Momma's help. But Aunt Maria said that she would take charge for me, and I am very grateful!

September 7, 1854

Dear Diary,

True to her word, Aunt Maria arrived bright and early and assisted me in getting prepared. It was a crazy day, but I always enjoy it. I love being around people and knowing that we are bringing in a bountiful harvest makes me even gladder. So much happened today that I can't even begin to describe it all. Overall, I am very thankful for all the friends we have been blessed with. As I looked out, it seemed like more people were here than at the others that I have been to. My guess is that it is because of Momma's death. Everyone wanted to come to support us.

September 8, 1854

Dear Diary,

Today there was a harvest at the Brown's house, but I stayed home today because I felt like I had to tidy up the place from yesterday. Poppa said he didn't mind, for he remembered Momma doing the same thing. Everyone else went though, and for once I enjoyed the quiet.

After cleaning the house, I sat down to do some sewing that needed to be done. It also was a good time to think about the upcoming winter that was speedily approaching and everything that must be done to prepare for that. But at this moment, I wasn't going to overwhelm myself.

September 9, 1854

Dear Diary,

There was a harvest at the Kulp's house today, and I went along with Poppa, Jesse, and the girls. Kirsten and I had gone out to bring water to the workers, but we ran out half way through, so I headed back for some more. As I was drawing the bucket up from the well, Cole Brown tapped me on the shoulder. I looked at him warily, sure that nothing he could say would be good. But instead of saying anything, he pushed me aside and finished my task for me.

"Thank you," I managed to stutter out. Cole gave me a sort of smile, but it didn't look genuine to me. Then he walked away without another word. I was completely shocked by his behavior. No crude words? No insulting snickers? I wanted to believe that he changed, but something deep down told me he didn't. But that still didn't explain his actions.

September 10, 1854

Dear Diary,

Today we went to the Harp's, and I must confess something...I kind of like Scott Harp. He's one of Jesse's good friends, so perhaps I just see him a lot. But he is very compassionate to kids, a hard worker, and respectful to adults. He can even joke around when the time is right. I think the spark just happened today, because I don't think I felt this way before. How I wish I could tell Momma what I am feeling. She would know what to say to me.

September 11, 1854

Dear Dairy,

Today, Reverend Mast spoke about wisdom and sort of tied it in with the harvest that has been going on. He read to us from James 3:13-18, but I shall record here verses 17 and 18. *"But the wisdom from above is first pure, then peaceable, gentle, open to reason, full of mercy and good fruits, impartial and sincere. And a harvest of righteousness is sown in peace by those who make peace."* Reverend Mast said that just like we have harvested our crops, we must also grow and harvest fruits within us; such as peace, patience, righteousness, love, kindness, and much more. He said that just like planting our corn seeds and watering and waiting for them to grow, we must water and wait for our fruits to grow inside of us and then we can harvest an abundance of those things.

September 12, 1854

Dear Dairy,

We went over to the Miller's today. Even though her husband passed away, Mrs. Miller decided to stay in her house and just hire someone to do the majority of the work for her crop. Somehow she needed to be provided for. Money doesn't just grow on trees, Poppa always tells me.

September 13, 1854

Dear Diary,

Today we went to the Bow's. Herbert and Hank Bow are two more of Jesse's friends, and they also have a sister Heather, who is a year older than me. Mrs. Bow is a very kind lady and she used to be good friends with Momma. When I was passing through the kitchen, Mrs. Bow pulled me aside and said that if there was anything I needed or wanted to talk about, she was more than happy to help. I thanked her with a smile and told her that I would let her know if I ever needed anything.

September 14, 1854

Dear Diary,

Poppa, Jesse, and Laura went to the Tailor's today. Bethy wasn't feeling that great, so she stayed home and I tended to her. I didn't really mind at all. Even though it is enjoyable, it does get tiring to go somewhere every day. But, it is the neighborly thing to do and it only happens once a year.

September 15, 1854

Dear Diary,

Poppa says that this will be the last harvest. Now
don't get me wrong, there are many more people in our
community, but there are often a couple harvests a day and
you just choose which ones to go to.

Today we went to the Rice's and because Bethy was
feeling better, we all went.

September 16, 1854

Dear Diary,

I can hardly believe that everyone has brought all
their crops in and now it is time to get ready for winter. We
have to preserve food (which we have been doing), go to
town for last minute supplies, get the house ready, chop
wood, and get the barn ready. One thing we have learned
since living in Minnesota is that you never know when the
first snow will arrive and it is always good to be prepared for
it.

September 17, 1854

Dear Diary,

Poppa allowed just Jesse and me to go to town today. He said that he didn't need anything and I wanted to pick up some things for the girls without them seeing it. It was nice just being with my brother. We have such different lives now that we don't get much of a chance for talking. "This trip reminds me of one we made with Momma back in the spring." I mentioned to Jesse, glancing over at him while I said it, but he just stared straight ahead. I figured he didn't want to talk about Momma, so I didn't say anything else.

I was surprised when he said, "It seems like forever since that happened."

I clasped my hands together and looked out too. "Do you talk to her? I mean like sometimes, I'll ask her things when I'm baking or sewing and I can almost imagine she's here."

Jesse looked over at me then. "You were the closest with her, not quite like the rest of us." I looked back over at Jesse. From the wistfulness of his voice, he sounded like he wished he would've spent more time with her. At least he probably visited her grave. I still can't bring myself to do it.

When we got to the general store, Jesse said he would
wait outside. I picked up some thick, woolen material for new
coats for Poppa and Jesse, and also some red and blue calico
to make dresses for Bethy and Laura. In addition to my fabric,
I picked up yarn and some grocery items.

We also made a stop at the post office, and I ran inside
to mail some letters to Sweden. I was very glad to see that I
had received one from *Mormor* for myself and also one from
her for the rest of the family.

When I got home, I went up to my room to read my
letter. It said:

Dear Carolyn,

*My heart aches after the sad news you have just written us
about your mother. I must tell you that I have cried for days after
your letter arrived. Hard times happen to us all, but I know you will
stay strong. You have always had your mother's spirit... Don't
forget to always trust in God and have faith...*

Her letter was much longer, too long to fit in my
diary. Her words brought tears to my eyes. Just knowing that
Mormor thought I had Momma's spirit made me smile. How I
long to see her and have her comfort me. But Sweden is too
far away for such frivolities!

September 18, 1854

Dear Diary,

Reverend Mast talked about how we can always run into God's arms and we will be safe. He will never turn us away or forsake us. Psalm 29:25 says, "*The fear of man lays a snare, but whoever trusts in the Lord is safe.*" God is our protector and Lord. If we are afraid of him, we will get caught; but if we trust the Lord, we are safe.

After the service, Mrs. Bow invited us over to her house for dinner. I gratefully accepted. When I told Poppa and my siblings, Poppa was fine with going and the girls were excited, but Jesse seemed to make no expression. "Don't you want to go, Jesse?" I asked him quietly before we left. He just shrugged and climbed up next to Bethy and Laura in the back of the wagon. I jumped up next to Poppa and we were on our way.

Dinner was very delicious, and afterwards I went back in the kitchen to help Mrs. Bow and Heather clean up. They insisted that I didn't have to, but I was so used to doing it, it came naturally. While I was drying, Mrs. Bow asked, "So, Carolyn, how have you been doing?" Her face showed true concern and I knew it just wasn't someone trying to do their duty.

I gave a half-shrug. "Okay. I'm moving into a routine now, so it's getting easier." I paused, not sure how much I wanted to say and how much I wanted to keep to myself. Heather had left the kitchen and Mrs. Bow looked at me, as if she knew that I had more to say. I decided it would be good to tell someone, and Mrs. Bow was one of Momma's closest friends. "I've never visited her grave. When Poppa buried her, I stayed inside with Jesse and Laura because they were still ill. I haven't been able to bring myself to go see it. I don't know, I guess I feel somewhat guilty yet. I know Poppa said not to, and that I did everything I could, but somewhere in me, I feel like I should've done more. I should've gotten help. I didn't know what to do. Poppa and Aunt Maria said that I did everything that anyone would've done. But I don't believe that. I didn't know everything. I just..." I couldn't go on, and I started crying. It felt good to get all that out. I couldn't even write it down. It just bottled up until it exploded in Mrs. Bow's kitchen.

Mrs. Bow walked over to me and placed an arm around my shoulder. "I'm not going to try to convince you anymore that it wasn't your fault. That's something that you need to accept on your own. I don't know what you are going through. I never lost close kin, only infant siblings that I never bonded with. If I were you, I would go to your mother's grave. Talk to her there. I think it will help you come to a peace of mind that she is really gone, and it wasn't your fault. I also think you should talk to your father about your feelings, and maybe your siblings. They might be going through the same thing. No matter what you decide to do, pray and trust God. He can relieve you from all your guilt. Times will get better, Carolyn. And your mother taught you so much." She smiled down at me and I was glad that I talked to her. Her answer to my problem sounded just like something Momma would say.

I smiled at her through my tears, "Thank you, Mrs. Bow."

"Anytime, Carolyn; and whenever you need to talk, you can come over."

September 19, 1854

Dear Diary,

I decided to do some baking today, and Bethy joined me. I decided to ask her about Momma. "How are you coping with Momma's death?"

She didn't take her eyes from the pie crust she was rolling. "I don't know. I guess, well, I didn't do a lot. You did all the work. I didn't know how. If you would've gotten sick, I'm sure we all would've died."

I looked over at my younger sister, shocked. Bethy felt guilty too? Why didn't I go to her earlier? I didn't think anyone felt the same as me. I left the cake I was mixing and walked over to her. "Bethy, you did so much. I couldn't have done it without you. Actually, I was feeling guilty myself. Many people have told me not to be, but Mrs. Bow told me that it is something we have to work through ourselves. And I'm sure we wouldn't have all died. You would've known what to do. It's like instinct. It just comes." I reached out and gave her a hug. Here I was concerned for me, and I wasn't helping my sisters deal through Momma's death at all. Why didn't I think they would grieve too?

September 20, 1854

Dear Dairy,

I took Laura with me when I went to the woods to pick some herbs. I thought perhaps that it might be a good time to talk about Momma with her. She didn't seem to answer any of my questions though. Maybe she is not grieving as much as I expected. Since she was ill herself, she had no guilt. We finished picking and headed back to the house. We were just passing the barn, when Laura asked, "Can I take some mint and put it on Momma's grave? She always loved mint leaves." I quickly nodded my head, and watched her disappear around the barn. Why wouldn't I follow her? I didn't know, so I quickly went inside.

September 21, 1854

Dear Diary,

This afternoon, Bethy and Laura went over to the Harp's to play with their best friends, Caddie and Julie. Poppa was out chopping wood, and I wasn't sure where Jesse was. Gathering up all of my courage, I determined that I would go out to Momma's grave. I couldn't be afraid any longer. I grabbed my shawl, for a chilly wind was brewing, and headed outside. I rounded the barn, and saw a mound of fresh dirt and a small wooden cross that stuck up from one end. The cross read: *Juliana Cradle Woodsmall. 1817-1854. Beloved wife, mother, and daughter.*

Tears gathered in my eyes, and I dropped to my knees on the dirt. "Oh, Momma, I'm so sorry for everything! I wish I could've saved you. I wish you were still here. I wish......" I couldn't say anymore. My tears were cascading down my face, and the words were getting stuck in my throat. I lay down on her grave and just cried. Pretty soon, I was starting to get wet, but I couldn't tell if it was my tears or the rain.

Someone placed a hand on my shoulder, but I didn't move. "Carrie," Jesse said. "Carrie, are you okay?" I could tell that he was worried about me, so I slowly sat up. My dress was covered with mud, for it was truly raining, and my face was streaked with dirt from crying.

"No," I managed to choke out. I started crying again, and Jesse came closer to me and wrapped his arms around me. "I didn't know it would hurt this bad," I muttered into his shirt. He just rocked me and held me tighter. When my tears lessened, I moved away and rubbed my face with my shawl that miraculously didn't get muddy. "Thank you."

He shrugged. "I did the same thing when I came here a couple weeks ago."

I gave him a sad smile, and he helped me stand.

We heard a horse riding up. "Not now," I groaned, but Jesse just smiled at me. When we came around the barn, I saw that it was Scott Harp.

"Scott!" Jesse cried and moved toward him. I stayed back, hoping he wouldn't see me.

Scott hopped down from his horse and told Jesse, "Your sisters want to spend the night, and my mother told me to come ask you."

Both of them then looked over at me, and I nodded. "Sure."

"Hey, you want to come in for a bit?" Jesse asked his friend.

Scott agreed, and the boys headed to the house. I followed, still not believing that Jesse would do such a thing to me. After making sure that they took their boots off on the porch and didn't make a muddy mess inside, I hurried upstairs to clean up. The one day I happen to look a mess is when Scott Harp shows up. Nevertheless, I was determined not to let that stop me from being the perfect hostess.

Stepping into the kitchen, I tried to figure out what I would make for supper. I didn't know if Scott was staying or not, but just in case, I must have plenty. Jesse and Scott ended up playing checkers, and when Poppa got home, he invited him to stay for supper.

After supper, I went up to my room to think about all that had happened today, mainly at Momma's grave. Something changed within me. I really, truly know that she is gone now. Somehow, it doesn't hurt as much now after I got all my emotions out. Mrs. Bow was right, visiting a grave really does help.

September 22, 1854

Dear Diary,

It is still raining today. I wish it wasn't, because I had wanted to go visit Kirsten, but had no desire to get wet like I did last night. Instead, I decided to write some more in my book. With the girls still at the Harp's and Jesse and Poppa outside, the house was quiet.

The next part of my book was our experience in New York City. I must say, I don't believe I like the city at all. It is so noisy and, shall I say, rude. I have never seen so many people trying to nudge ahead in line, and knock us around. It was especially unsettling because we didn't understand what many people were saying. That night in the boarding house was just as bad. The building was right next door to a bar and it was very loud! Kirsten and I shared a bed, and I'm not quite sure we ever fell asleep. The next morning, we boarded a train that would take us to Minnesota.

I put aside my writing once the girls came home. After I helped them change out of their wet clothes, Bethy helped me make supper.

September 23, 1854

Dear Diary,

The sun was shining brightly today, so I decided to take advantage of it and ride over and visit Kirsten. I found her sitting outside, so I joined her. We talked for quite some time, until Kirsten finally asked me, "How are you dealing with your mother's death, Carolyn?"

I turned to her and answered quite honestly, "If you

would've asked me that a week ago, I would've said not very well. But now, I don't know, something's changed; for the better. I think I've finally come to terms with her death."

She smiled at me. "I know sort of what you mean. Herb died while I was sick, and I just don't remember ever being sad or worried. The whole cholera just blew over me. It was really shocking when I found out that he and Aunt Juliana had died. And then the shock turns to utter sadness. You know?"

I nodded. We both had experienced our grief; me during the cholera and she after. It was nice to sit and talk with her again, and even now, I think it helps me to know that others are grieving. I don't know why, but it does.

September 24, 1854

Dear Diary,

Poppa took Bethy and Laura into town today with him, and while they were gone, I decided to do some mopping. Ever since those rainy days, the floor has been very muddy and then the mud dries and it is dirty. Cleaning is not what I would call my favorite task, but it has to be done sometime.

Once I finished my cleaning, Poppa came back and brought a letter with him. It was addressed to all of us from *Farmor*. So after dinner, I read aloud the letter, like Momma always used to do. It said:

Dear family,

The news about Juliana has struck us deeply, and we are very sorry to hear about it. Likewise, your grandfather has just recently died. The doctor says from old age, but really, he wasn't doing very well. Since his death, I have decided to move in with Kathy. I do so hope that the cholera is now over, for I do not want any more of my family to die.

Love, Farmor Kathy

After I finished reading *Farmor's* letter, it struck me how different they can be. *Mormor* writes heart-felt personal letters to each of us, whereas *Farmor* writes one letter for the whole family. I don't think that *Farmor* loves us any less, it's just her personality.

I do wish though that *Mormor* and Grandpa would come to America. I think *Mormor* would want to, but Grandpa always says that he doesn't want to leave Sweden. He will live and die in the place of his ancestors. *Farmor* will not leave because Kathy, her only daughter, lives in Sweden and she does not want to come either. I'm aching for a letter from

Millie, but I shall just have to wait and continue to write her.

September 25, 1854

Dear Diary,

Reverend Mast read from Lamentations 3:22-24. It says, *"The steadfast love of the Lord never ceases; his mercies are new every morning; great is your faithfulness. 'The Lord is my portion,' says my soul, 'therefore I will hope in him.'"* It comforts me to know that the Lord will never stop loving me, no matter what I do. He gives us a fresh chance at the break of every day. God is enough to satisfy, if only we give him everything and let him be enough.

September 26, 1854

Dear Diary,

I decided to go out on a ride today. It is always refreshing for me to go out on a ride in God's creation. Laura begged for me to take her along too, so I did. Laura loves the outdoors even more than I do. It was a special time for me to share with her.

As we were passing through the woods, Cole Brown came riding past. Laura turned to me, anger in her eyes at what he might say to us. I wasn't quite sure myself, for last time I saw him, he helped me with my bucket of water. He passed with a nod of his head.

After he passed, Laura asked me what I thought of that. I shrugged; I really couldn't make him out. I asked Laura, "Why did you look the way you did? You needn't be angry at him."

Laura sighed. "If he had said anything bad about you, I was going to fight him."

I smiled, "I'm sure you were." The image of my baby sister fighting Cole Brown was almost amusing.

Laura didn't think it was funny. "I was, Carolyn. I heard the bad things Sherry said about you in school and at the harvests. If he was of the same mind, he was in for it."

I froze. "What did she say about me?" Laura eyed me warily as if she was wondering whether or not to tell me. "Laura, tell me," I commanded in a strict voice.

"Well, she said that she always knew your type. That you didn't want to learn and were waiting to drop out of school, so that you could pretend that you were better than them; more adult. And then at the harvests, she said that you were acting even more an adult, because you helped in the kitchen and didn't play with the children. Though I'm not

79

sure why she would call herself a child, but anyway, I'm sure he is of the same mind. They always teased us before, about our Swedish heritage, and he was always the bulk of that teasing. I'm not sure why he's nice to you. But I wouldn't trust him." Her eyes were large as she relayed to me the matter of such importance.

I couldn't believe what I was hearing. My schoolmates were really saying that about me? "Well, you can tell them next time, that I would love to be in school, but I am only obeying my mother's last wishes." I wasn't quite sure if Laura would really say that, but she smiled at me.

As we rode home, I couldn't help but continue to think about what Laura had told me. Did Bethy know? And Kirsten? Probably, but they didn't want to hurt me. Oh, my little Laura, she always stuck up for people, especially her family and friends.

September 27, 1854

Dear Diary,

I wanted to make a raisin nut cake today, which is one of Poppa's favorite cakes. While I made that, Bethy started making some bread. Of course, I honored her with a story of my own. This story was about when I was a young girl living in Sweden.

"When I was about five, Momma decided to take me visiting with her. Usually, she left me with *Mormor* when she would go on her weekly visits, but this time, she decided to bring me along. Of course, I was very excited about the prospect of going. I dressed in my best outfit, even though Momma told me to put something on that was a little less fancy.

"Pretty soon, we were off down the road. Our first stop was Mrs. Henderson's. She tended to be a larger lady, and she always had a couple of cookie jars filled with different kinds of cookies. Momma allowed me to have two, and so I ate them as politely as I could while Momma visited. As we were leaving, I snuck a couple more cookies. I knew it was very disobedient, but they were delicious, and I reasoned that I would share with Jesse.

"We continued our visiting, and at our last stop, I was not feeling very good. My stomach was so unsettled, and I had sharp pains. Momma had to take me home, but first we had to go by *Mormor's* and pick up Jesse, Laura, and you. Momma told *Mormor* that I must've picked something up, but she didn't know what because it came on all of a sudden.

Mormor took one look at me and said, 'Well, Juliana, she's not sick. She has a very bad stomachache.' Momma looked down at me, and instantly figured out that it must've been all those cookies I had eaten at Mrs. Henderson's. After that day, I never ate more than two cookies in a day." I smiled at Bethy, and she laughed.

"I can't imagine you being so greedy, Carolyn." That brought more laughter from both of us.

September 28, 1854

Dear Diary,

Jesse and Scott had gone on a ride this morning, and until they came back, I didn't know they had been in town. I was outside getting some firewood for my stove in the kitchen, when they came galloping into the yard.

Jesse had a mischievous grin on his face. "Carrie, I have a surprise for you!"

"Really? Are you carrying this wood in for me?"

Jesse looked like he might topple off his horse from his excitement, "A letter came for you...from Millie." He pulled it out of his pocket and waved it at me.

I screamed, dropped my wood, and ran over to him,

yanking the letter out of his hand. When it was in my possession, I ran inside to read it.

"What about the wood?" Jesse called after me, but I didn't care about the wood one bit.

Once I reached my room, I tore the letter open. How I have waited for a letter from my dear cousin. She wrote:

My dear Carolyn,

I'm dreadfully sorry that I have not written earlier. I must confess, I have no reason at all for not writing. Farmor has told me about your mother, and I'm so sorry to hear that. I'm sure you must be feeling a terrible loss. Momma sends her love as well, and says that now she will treasure Aunt Juliana's last letter more than ever.

How I wish I could come and see you! It would be wonderful to talk face to face. I can't believe you left only four years ago. I suppose a letter can satisfy a little, though I would love to see you.

I suppose you have heard about Grandpa's death. Farmor misses him dreadfully; I can see it in her eyes. She is now living with Aunt Kathy, Uncle Cain, and Charity.

Have I told you that George has a girlfriend? Her name is Phoebe and she is very sweet. Phoebe doesn't have any sisters either, so we are a perfect fit! Sometimes she will come over just to hang out with me, even when George isn't around.

Amos is just as annoying as ever. You are very lucky not to have a younger brother, Carolyn. The last letter you wrote to me, I placed on the desk in my room. Next thing I knew, he was running around the house, waving it in his hands. Thankfully, he didn't read any and Momma punished him for going into my room and taking something that was mine.

I shall try to be more faithful, like you, in my letter writing. Until then, I am ever your loving cousin,

Millie

Millie's letter thrilled me to no end. How I love getting caught up on news from Sweden. I am so glad that Millie now has Phoebe. Before we left, she said that I was always her sister. Kirsten, Millie, and I always called ourselves "cousin-sisters."

When I went back downstairs, I found that my kitchen fire had died from the lack of wood. Where was Jesse anyways? Where was anyone? Didn't anyone know how to run a household? Going outside, I found Jesse and Scott high up in one of our trees, eating apples.

I looked up and asked, "Where are Bethy and Laura?"

Jesse shrugged, "Beats me. How is Millie?"

Ignoring his question, I asked, "You could've at least put wood in the kitchen stove. Now my fire is out, and supper will be extra late."

Jesse gave Scott a look, then he said, "Okay, okay. Well, maybe you should've waited to read your letter until after you put wood in the stove."

I was about to say something, but Scott interrupted me. "You know, you could all come over to our house for supper. Your sisters are most likely there, if they're not here."

I was about to refuse, when Jesse accepted. Resigned to the fact, I headed to find Poppa and tell him we were going to the Harp's for supper. I hated to impose on other people, especially now that I was a housekeeper myself.

To my utter surprise, Poppa wasn't in the barn. "Where is everyone?" I asked aloud. This was turning a bit ridiculous. Jesse and Scott came in the barn. "Ready to go, Carrie?" Jesse asked me.

I turned around. "Where is Poppa?"

Jesse started laughing. "How is it possible that you lose everybody? I knew I should've kept that letter from you."

Now it was Scott who started laughing. "That is not true one bit, Jesse Woodsmall. We had to ride home as fast as we could in order to get that letter home to Carolyn."

Jesse looked sheepish, but he was finally defeated. "Leave him a note, and we can ride over to the Harp's awhile."

I was uncertain. "Maybe I should wait here..."

Jesse seemed exasperated. "Please, Carolyn. It will be fine. Get your horse."

I started walking out of the barn. "You get it. I need to write a note to Poppa and the girls telling them what's happening, make sure all the lamps are off, and get the cake I just made to bring along."

"How are you planning on riding with a cake?" Jesse called after me, but I didn't answer him; let him figure it out for himself.

Let me just say, Jesse was right; it was very hard riding with a cake. Luckily for me, I convinced the boys to walk, not run, the horses. On our way, we met up with Poppa, who had stopped by to see Uncle Levi. After I told him what had happened, he joined us on our trek.

Mrs. Harp was not put out at all for us coming over, and she said herself that she had been planning on inviting us soon. Bethy and Laura were indeed here, playing with Caddie and Julie. Supper was very good, and in the end, I'm almost glad Jesse didn't keep the fire going.

September 29, 1854

Dear Diary,

I decided to write in my book some more. The next chapter in our journey would be the train ride from New York to Minnesota. Let's just say that it was not pleasant at all. It was December and very, very cold to ride in a train with no heat. There was even a layover in Ohio, because it was snowing and we couldn't move. That was another situation. Here we were, heading to Minnesota, where we knew of other Swedish immigrants, but here, we knew no one. We all decided to just stay on the train, but soon we needed some food, because the train wouldn't serve while we were on hold. Poppa decided to go out and I went with him, just to see some more of America. It was not quite what I expected. It was a very out-of-the-way town, with not much there at all. We had a hard time finding food, because most of the stores were closed and the street venders had put their stands away because of the snow. We knocked on a couple doors, but no one could understand us, or tried to. We trudged back to the train, and since we still didn't move by evening, the train provided us with food. By mid-afternoon the next day, we were on our way, again.

September 30, 1854

Dear Diary,

I decided to do some wash today. After convincing Laura to help me, we began the backbreaking task of wash day. We filled our tub with water from the well, and then scrubbed it hard with the scrub board and soap. After that, it went into a different tub to be rinsed, and then finally, we hung it up. It is much nicer with three people, but Bethy was inside sewing and I know how much she dislikes this job.

After Laura and I finished, we sat down on the front porch steps with a glass of water and a cookie. I sighed contentedly and looked out at our land. "It's so beautiful in September. The leaves are changing and everything is preparing itself for winter."

Laura was silent for a moment, and then asked, "What do you think Momma's doing?"

I turned to my little sister. "What?"

"What do you think she is doing? Can she see us?" Laura asked.

I didn't know what to say. "Of course she can see us. God does, and I'm sure Momma can." We didn't say anything more, just then. Silence was enough. I had enough to think about. What was Momma doing? Was she singing with the angels? Was she walking on the streets of gold? Could she see Herb and Grandpa Woodsmall? Could she see both us and *Mormor* at the same time? I know God can, but can Momma? I can't even beginning to imagine what it will be like. What will heaven be like?

October 1, 1854

Dear Diary,

I rode over to visit Kirsten today. I wanted to tell her all about Millie's letter, and also ask her if the rumors about me were true. Kirsten was so excited that I heard from Millie, and I gave her the letter to read over. After she read it, I asked her again about what Sherry was spreading about me. Kirsten sighed. "I didn't tell you before, because I knew you wouldn't like it, and why hurt you anymore? And secondly, I'm sure she's only jealous of you. She probably wishes she were at least half as pretty as you. But don't pay her any mind. It's just her and Cole who say that stuff." That sort of put my mind at ease, knowing that no one else was saying such things.

October 2, 1854

Dear Diary,

Reverend Mast was preaching on God's promises today. Isaiah 25:1 says, *"O Lord, I will honor and praise Your name, for You are my God. You do such wonderful things! You planned them long ago, and now You have accomplished them."* God knew long ago what he was going to do, and everything has happened according to his plan. It is a comfortable feeling to know that God has a purpose and plan for everything. He knew Momma would die from cholera and he knows that we will be able to manage without her. It might be difficult at some times, but God has everything already worked out.

October 3, 1854

Dear Diary,

We received word today that school would be starting back up again on Monday. It is hard to believe that I will be on my own again and I will not be going to school with my siblings and friends. Even Jesse is going this time and it will be his last year. It is going to be so quiet around the house, but maybe I'll be able to get a lot of writing done!

October 4, 1854

Dear Diary,

Poppa let me take the wagon into town today. I had thought he was letting me go alone, but then when I went outside, Jesse was sitting there. I should've known better. My Poppa still thinks of me as his little Carrie. Nevertheless, I did enjoy my ride with Jesse. He's not one who likes to talk a lot, but I did the talking. I told him about my letter from Millie, and that I was writing a book about our trip for Sweden. After I said it, I made him promise he wouldn't tell anyone. I hadn't planned on telling anyone about it, but it just sort of came out because I was so excited.

When we got to town, I did my usual shopping at the general store and stopped at the post office to mail my weekly letters to *Mormor, Farmor,* and Millie. There were no letters for us today, and I was a little disappointed.

On our way back, we drove by Mrs. Miller's house and I saw her on the front porch. Jesse stopped the wagon, and we had a brief conversation with her. I invited her for supper on the seventh, and she said she would be glad to come. Something in me enjoys having company over and making big dinners. Momma did too; I'm sure I got that love of cooking from her and *Mormor*.

October 5, 1854

Dear Diary,

In preparation for my company coming in two days, I decided to clean the house today. I assigned Bethy to the upstairs, Laura would do the dusting downstairs, and I would do the mopping downstairs. Moving very swiftly and efficiently, my sisters and I finished the task right before lunch. Once we ate lunch, Bethy and I sat down to do some sewing and mending, and Laura went outside to help Poppa stack the wood pile.

When Jesse, Poppa, and Laura came in for supper, Poppa said that he ran into Mr. Bow while he was out chopping wood this morning and invited their family to come for supper on the seventh. I stared at him, astonished, "Poppa, the Millers are coming on the seventh."

Poppa continued eating. "Then you'll just have an extra big party."

I stared at Poppa, and I could feel Laura and Bethy's looks of astonishment. Oh dear! What did I say about loving parties?

October 6, 1854

Dear Diary,

Bethy and I decided to get a head start in the kitchen, preparing food for tomorrow's meal. Laura pleaded to be allowed to help Poppa and Jesse outside, and I let her, but said that she must help tomorrow. We made a blueberry pie, raspberry-chocolate cake, and three loaves of bread today. In addition to the food for tomorrow, we also made beef and cabbage soup for supper tonight and lunch tomorrow. Even though it is a lot of work and not what I had expected, I do enjoy cooking. I especially enjoy it when people praise my cooking. I don't mean to be vain, but it is so nice to be praised.

October 7, 1854

Dear Diary,

Today my sisters and I had a lot of preparing to do. This morning, I put Bethy in charge cutting all the potatoes, and Laura did the carrots. I prepared the roast, and then I put them all in a pan and placed it in our oven. Next, I sent Laura and Bethy to the ice house, which is located between our house and Uncle Levi's, to get some ice. While they were gone, I did a quick tidy-up of the house. Then it was lunch, and we all ate the leftover soup from last night.

After lunch, Bethy and I arranged the table to make sure it was set long enough, and Laura went down to the cellar to get the red beets, applesauce, and raspberry jam. Bethy and Laura set the table, while I figured out what serving bowls to put everything in. By the time everyone got here, all the food was on the table, and we were ready for our guests.

Mrs. Miller and Mrs. Bow both said that Bethy, Laura, and I did a wonderful job with the meal. After supper was over and we had dessert, Heather came into the kitchen to help me clean up. It was nice talking to her, since I don't usually have the chance to. She told me that she would miss me this coming term at school, but she said that she would do the same thing if she were in my shoes. I knew what she was referring to me staying home and minding the house since Momma died and it meant a lot to me to hear her say it. When we finished cleaning up, we joined everyone else in the main room by the fire. It turned out to be a very lovely dinner.

October 8, 1854

Dear Diary,

After the last few days, I was glad to just sit down and do some sewing that I had been meaning to do. I was trying to knit a blanket for this coming winter, but it was a slow process. I was never really fond of knitting. But, Momma always made a new blanket every winter. She said, "It's good to always have blankets. One can never have too many, and this is one item that you can't just whip up if there is a hole somewhere." Now I know what she meant by that!

October 9, 1854

Dear Diary,

Reverend Mast spoke today about obedience and sacrifice. 1 Samuel 15:22 says, "*Obedience is better than sacrifice, and submission is better than offering the fat rams.*" Reverend Mast said that while it is good to give our tithes to God, what he wants even more is to give ourselves. Obeying him in everything is better than anything we could possibly have to sacrifice.

October 10, 1854

Dear Diary,

Jesse, Bethy, and Laura went back to school today. I didn't truly know how lonely I would be till after they left. Poppa was also gone; he went out to the woods and was chopping wood all day.

With everyone gone, I decided to take advantage of the quiet and write some more of my book. We had just arrived in Minnesota, and it wasn't like any of us had imagined it to be. From the train station, Mr. and Mrs. Holbrook met us with a wagon and transported us to our farm, which was about an hour away. Mr. and Mrs. Holbrook were originally from Sweden, but they moved to America about three years previous to when we did. Mr. Holbrook and Poppa were good friends, and he sent many letters to Poppa telling him of how wonderful the land was. As we were driving from the station, we passed through a little town, which is our town now. It was about the same size as it is now, though I think the population has grown a bit. Pretty soon we reached our land. There was a little cabin sitting right where our house is now, and the six of us moved in. Then Mr. Holbrook took Uncle Levi's family about a half a mile away, where there was also a little cabin for them. We lived in that first cabin all through that winter, spring, and summer. In the fall, Poppa harvested a good crop, and he was able to build us the house we have now. We have much to be thankful for, for God has provided all our needs.

October 11, 1854

Dear Diary,

I did some sewing today. For Christmas, I am planning on making Bethy and Laura new church dresses, so now is the perfect time to work on them since they are at school. In addition to the dresses, I also worked a little bit on the blanket that I am knitting. I am determined to add a little every day.

While I was sewing, I imagined Momma sitting in her favorite rocking chair across from me. It was so vivid a vision, that I began talking to her. I told her about the book I was writing, and about the letters I had received from *Mormor* and *Farmor* and Millie. Then I told her how well Laura and Bethy were doing in helping me with the housework, and that they were both enjoying school. I mentioned that Poppa and Jesse are working very hard outside, and I said how we all miss her so much. Suddenly, I heard the door open.

Poppa walked in. He stared at me for a second and then asked, "Who were you talking to?"

I looked at him, and then back down at my knitting. "Momma." I knew it was all a dream now, and that she really wasn't sitting across from me. But talking to her had freed up my mind.

October 12, 1854

Dear Diary,

Today, I decided to do some baking. I made a couple loaves of bread and a strawberry rhubarb pie. In addition to that, I also made some chicken noodle soup, which would be for our supper. It is still surprising to me that I am the only one here. I keep thinking that Bethy or Laura will run in the door and tell me something that just happened, or that Jesse will come in looking for a piece of bread or pie. I'm glad that Poppa always comes in for lunch though. I always make sure that I have something ready for him.

October 13, 1854

Dear Diary,

This morning, I sat down at my little desk upstairs in my loft and decided to write more of my book.

We have just arrived in Minnesota, in the middle of December. You can probably imagine that this is not a good scenario. Shortly after we arrived, a large blizzard came up. Poppa had to brave out and find us some firewood, because we had none. Luckily, the day before, we went into town and got some provisions, so we had food, and Momma had packed plenty of blankets from Sweden to keep us nice and warm. Even though there was a blizzard howling around us, I think that was one of the nicest times we had. We were all together, and we shared stories as we snuggled by the fire. I remember sitting on the floor, wrapped up in a blanket with Bethy, as we listened to Poppa read from the Bible.

October 15, 1854

Dear Diary,

Poppa rode into town today, and when he returned he brought a letter from *Mormor*. I have been longing for a letter from her for so long now! It said:

My dearest Carolyn,

Your last letter brought me much comfort. I am so relieved that you have visited your momma's grave after weeks of feeling guilt and regret. I have often heard that laying everything before God truly does help a person to get over those feelings. I'm sure you have already done that, but I wanted to remind you just the same.

Your grandpa is keeping very busy around here. He and Mort are very much into making little wood carvings these days. Even though he seems to be as healthy and vibrant as ever, I can start to see some weakness that comes with old age.

Kale's wedding was a wondrous occasion. Marie made a lovely bride. How I wish your family and Levi's could've seen it. Your Uncle Kaleb and Aunt Marylou looked so proud, as were your grandpa and I. It was wonderful to have such a happy time, after the death of your dear mother and Herb.

Before I close, I wanted to leave you with a scripture. Psalm 55:16, 17, and 22 says, "But I call to God, and the Lord will save me. Evening and morning and at noon I utter my complaint and moan, and he hears my voice. Cast your burden on the Lord, and he will sustain you; he will never permit the righteous to be moved."

Always remember to call on the Lord. He will help you whenever you need him too, Carolyn. All my love and prayers.

Mormor

Mormor's letters are always filled with information about Sweden and also wisdom for me. The scripture she included was so helpful that I couldn't help but cry. These past few weeks, I have been praying morning, noon, and night. I was praying for Momma to be healed, then Jesse, Laura, and Poppa; and then I was praying for the hurt and guilt inside of me to go away. *Mormor* always knows what is really going on with me, even if I don't write it in my letters.

October 16, 1854

Dear Diary,

Reverend Mast read from Deuteronomy 6 about the greatest commandment. Verses 4 and 5 say, *"Here, O Israel: The Lord our God, the Lord is one. You shall love the Lord you God with all your heart and with all your soul and with all your might."* Reverend Mast told us that this is the greatest commandment in the whole Bible and Jesus himself preaches on it in the New Testament. As I began to think about it more, I can see why. God created us all and he even sent his only son to die on the cross to forgive us our sins. Why shouldn't he want us to love him above all else? It seems hard to do sometimes because really, I think I love my family more. But even if something happens, like Momma leaving me, God never leaves me and he will never stop loving me.

October 17, 1854

Dear Diary,

I decided to write some more of my story today. It seems as though Mondays are my writing day.

The next part of my story is the beginning of spring. The cold days are coming to a close and the days are getting longer and less cold. Because it is getting warmer, Momma has allowed Jesse and I to go on walks around our property. Bethy and Laura are too little to go, but I always promise to tell them everything about our adventures.

One day we were walking and we came across the stream which was near Uncle Levi and Aunt Maria's house. Jesse wanted to figure out a way to cross it because he wanted to explore the woods. Now the stream isn't usually deep, but because of all the recent snow melting, there was a heavy current. As Jesse walked around trying to find tree limbs to use as bridges, I sat at the edge and placed my toes in the water. We must have been there awhile for soon Kirsten, Luke, and Herb appeared. The boys instantly went to help

Jesse, but Kirsten sat with me. All too soon, it was time to head back, but it was agreed that the bridge building would commence the following day.

The next day, we all went out, but this time, brought with us some nails and a hammer. I thought they were a bit crazy, trying to build something when there were plenty of other new places to explore. By mid-morning, the "bridge" was complete. It consisted of two logs nailed together with smaller pieces standing upright on both sides to act as railing.

To this day, the bridge still stands, and it is very helpful in getting across the stream!

October 21, 1854

Dear Diary,

These past couple days have passed in such a blur, with me lying in bed. On the eighteenth, I had decided to go out to the ice house to get some ice because I wanted to make some ice cream to surprise my family. When I descended into the coldness, I left the door open with a brick as a prop, because the door locks from the outside once it is closed. This is in use to ensure the animals can't come in, or at least I think it is. All of a sudden, I heard a bang. I looked up and the door was shut. How could this happen? I didn't hear anybody up there and my brick couldn't move by itself. I ran up the stairs rapidly and started banging on the door, screaming for help. No one could hear my cries, or they pretended not to. I sat down on the top step and tried to think. Someone would come. I knew it. But how long would it take? If I stayed in too long, I might freeze. After a long while, I started to feel a little dizzy and then everything went black.

When I woke up a later, Jesse told me what happened after I had blacked out. He and Luke had also been hungry for ice cream, so after school, they decided to stop by the ice house to bring some ice to me and see if I would make it. Upon opening the door, they saw me lying on the floor. Kneeling by my side, they could feel that I was very cold, but still breathing. I was carried to Aunt Maria's who placed me in a bed and began warming me up. Jesse says that I had been delirious and had started calling for Momma. Everyone was worried about me. Poppa thought that I should be taken to the doctor, but Aunt Maria said that it was just a mild case of hypothermia. It was agreed that I would stay at Aunt Maria's for a bit, but I just was told that I could probably go back to my own bed in a couple of days. I am so glad. I almost miss doing all my household duties. I am also very glad Bethy brought over my diary. Just think of how awful it would be if I forgot everything that had just happened!

October 25, 1854

Dear Diary,

I know it has been a few days since I have last written, but I have been so weak and tired. Being as I am still in bed, Bethy stayed home from school to tend to me. Yes, I am back in my own bed and it feels ever so nice. I feel well enough to get back to doing my regular duties, but Poppa insists that I stay in bed for a couple more days. As Bethy sits in my bedroom with me, we begin talking about who could've possibly shut the door on me. It must have been someone, because it couldn't have shut on its own. But all the kids who might have thought it would be a silly prank were in school that day. It remains a mystery.

October 27, 1854

Dear Diary,

I was finally allowed out of bed today. After over a week in bed, you must imagine my relief. Though I'm still a little weak if I stand up too long, I decided to make some bread. My family must be starving, for I can't even imagine what they have been eating. In addition to the bread, I also put on a pot of beef stew and made raspberry pudding. When it was supper time, Jesse could hardly contain his excitement at the sight of the fresh bread!

October 28, 1854

Dear Diary,

It's time to give the house a good cleaning, so that is exactly what I did today. I thoroughly dusted and then mopped. Once Jesse and the girls got back from school, I gave Jesse and Laura the task of beating out the rugs and Bethy helped me with supper. Everything feels so good when it is all cleaned up and in its proper place.

October 29, 1854

Dear Diary,

Poppa and Jesse went into town today, and the girls and I did the wash. As a mentioned before, doing the wash is tedious work. I would've much rather gone with Poppa and Jesse into town. But, when they got home, a letter from *Farmor* had arrived.

At supper time, after we had finished eating, Poppa read aloud her letter. It said:

Dear George, Jesse, Carolyn, Bethany, and Laura,

I hope this letter finds you all in good health, as Carolyn's last one has found me. It is pretty cold here in Sweden and we have begun to have some heavy snowfalls. There is still no news as to a marriage between your cousin George and Phoebe. Melissa and I are praying that it happens, for Phoebe is truly a wonderful girl and is perfect for young George.

Millie, Amos, and Charity are as busy as ever with school. Millie has said that she is going to apply to be the teacher's assistant next term. I think that school teaching is a lovely ambition.

It seems now that I am living with Kathy, I have more time than ever on my hands because she doesn't allow me to cook or clean. That reminds me, I have included the recipe for the eggnog mixture on the back of this letter, Carolyn. I am glad you thought to ask me, for your dear mother did like to keep all her favorite recipes tucked in her head.

All my love,

Farmor

As soon as *Farmor* mentioned that she included the eggnog recipe, Poppa, Jesse, Bethy, and Laura begged me to make it. I promised I would, as soon as I found time!

107

October 30, 1854

Dear Diary,

This morning, Reverend Mast taught more on how we should love the Lord. The scripture he read from was Psalm 116:1-2, *"I love the Lord, because he has heard my voice and my pleas for mercy. Because he inclined his ear to me, therefore I will call on him as long as I live."* These verses pretty much sum up everything that I have been going through. When I called on God, he listened and answered me. It is like when God answers you and blesses you in ways that you couldn't even imagine; it just makes me want to serve him forever.

October 31, 1854

Dear Diary,

I decided to write some more in my book this morning. I have just gotten to the part when it was time to start the planting. Poppa had gone into town to purchase some seed and borrow a plow. As he plowed the field, Jesse, Momma, and I followed behind planting the seeds in the ground. Bethy and Laura watched from the edge of the field where they were playing with their dolls.

I can still remember that evening and how happy

Poppa looked after the crop was planted. It was a happy day
for all of us, for it was a start in our new home.

November 1, 1845

Dear Diary,

I decided to try my hand at making eggnog from the
recipe *Farmor* has sent me. It turned out okay, but it didn't
quite taste the way I remember when Momma made it. I
closed my eyes and tried to remember anything extra she
used to put in. Suddenly an image popped into my head of

being in the kitchen making eggnog with Momma. She was rattling off her recipe for me to gather the ingredients, and then she said, "Now, Carolyn, this is strictly a secret. Every time I make eggnog, I always put a dash of cinnamon in, for it helps enhance the flavor." I was so excited! I had remembered Momma's secret ingredient. After putting in a dash of cinnamon, the eggnog tasted perfect!

When Poppa got home, I gave him a glass. He drank it very slowly and then nodded his head, "Very nicely done, Carolyn. I see you figured out the secret ingredient."

I gave him a smile, "Of course, Poppa."

November 2, 1854

Dear Diary,

It began to snow soon after Jesse, Bethy, and Laura left for school. Since I knew they would be wet and cold when they got home, I made some beef stew and warm chocolate chip cookies. When they got home and the cookies were on the table, still steaming, Laura gave a little scream and ran over to them. They told me everything that was happening in school while we ate cookies. How I wish I could go! Even though I'm getting used to what I have to do every day, there is nothing like the feeling of going to school.

November 3, 1854

Dear Diary,

It is still snowing as of this morning. When Jesse, Bethy, and Laura left for school, there were fourteen inches on the ground. Poppa came in for lunch, and he asked me how everything was going.

"That's a pretty general question, Poppa."

He laughed. "All right then. How is the housekeeping coming along?"

I thought a bit, "It is going pretty well. I'm starting to enjoy it."

"Good, good." We talked a bit more about the weather and reminiscing about Sweden. It was nice just to talk with him.

November 4, 1854

Dear Diary,

The snow was letting up a little bit, but it was still coming down. Poppa caught a cold and stayed in bed today. I told him it was probably because he was working outside in the snow the past few days. He just laughed me off and said that he would work outside come rain or shine. I made him some of Momma's chicken corn soup, remembering every little thing that she would add to make it the most flavorful soup ever.

November 5, 1854

Dear Diary,

The snow has finally ceased and we now have about two and a half feet. Since it was Saturday, Bethy and Laura spent much of the day playing out in the snow. How I remember loving to do that, but I had to make supper or I would have a very unhappy family!

November 6, 1854

Dear Diary,

Tomorrow's Bethany's 10th birthday and after the church service, I invited Uncle Levi, Aunt Maria, Kirsten, and Luke for supper to celebrate. In the afternoon, I finished up a new dress and apron, which of course, I put off till the last minute.

Reverend Mast had preached again about love. This

time, it was on loving our enemies and our neighbors.

Matthew 5:44-45 says, "*I say to you, Love your enemies and pray for those who persecute you, so that you may be sons of your Father who is in heaven.*" We are all God's children, and he loves everyone. So if we consider ourselves his daughter or son, we are all brothers and sisters and we should love everyone.

November 7, 1854

Dear Diary,

Since it was Bethy's birthday dinner tonight, I cleaned the house this morning and then did some cooking and baking this afternoon. I made roasted chicken, potatoes, green beans, red beets, carrots, and bread. For dessert, I made a strawberry-chocolate cake. Aunt Maria is also bringing over oatmeal raisin cookies.

After school, Bethy and Laura helped me finish up in the kitchen as well as set the table for the dinner. When supper was finished, she opened her presents. Poppa gave her a new hat and hair ribbons, Laura and Jesse made a little kitchen set for her dolls, Aunt Maria, Uncle Levi, and Kirsten gave her some yarn, Luke carved some little horses, and I gave her a new dress and apron and Momma's sewing kit.

Our Bethy, being the ever thankful person that she is, went around and gave everyone a hug.

November 8, 1854

Dear Diary,

I decided to write today, since I just cleaned yesterday and had enough leftovers for supper tonight. The next part in my book is going to school. Even though I loved learning, going to school made me nervous because I didn't speak English very well. Bethy, Jesse, and my cousins would all be going too, which made me feel a little better. Our teacher's name was Miss Smith and she was very nice and patient. It didn't take Bethy long at all to learn English, but it took a couple weeks for the rest of us. After much practice at home though, and helping Momma and Poppa to learn as well, we soon were speaking it pretty well and were doing great at school.

November 10, 1854

Dear Diary,

Wash day today. It took all morning for me to do it all by myself, but I wanted to get it finished instead of waiting till the girls got home. In the afternoon, I decided to go over and visit Momma's grave for a little. I didn't do much talking, just sort of sat and thought. How different my life would be right now if Momma were here. For one thing, I wouldn't even be home. I would be at school learning with my siblings and friends. Also, I wouldn't have to do all of the work that is now required of me to do.

On the other hand, since Momma's death, I have come to learn a great many things. I learned all extra stuff that is required when cooking or cleaning. I think my reliance on God has also strengthened. He has seen me through so much these past couple months and instead of pushing him away because of my grief, I accepted his help and his love.

After pondering over all of that, I looked up and whispered, "Thank you." I'm not sure if that was aimed at God or Momma......maybe both.

November 11, 1854

Dear Diary,

I went for a ride on Lucia this morning. It is starting to get a little chillier, since we did have snow, but this morning was an exception. It was such a lovely morning. The leaves are now all off the trees and there are still some signs of snow on the ground. I caught sight of a lone squirrel racing about trying to find some more acorns before heavier snow drifts settled in. I love to go riding in all the different seasons and see how everything has changed.

November 12, 1854

Dear Diary,

Jesse, Laura, and I went into town today. They dropped me off at the general store and then told me they would pick me up in twenty minutes or so. I headed inside and picked up my grocery items first, and then I went to browse in the textile section. There were so many nice fabrics and I desperately wished I could buy some to make a new dress for myself or one of the girls. But such luxuries were not to be had. After picking up some cotton thread, I paid for my purchases and went outside to wait for Jesse and Laura. I was going to walk around a little, but after buying so much, I decided it best just to wait.

While I was waiting, Cole Brown appeared, sitting atop a very well-looking horse. He looked down at me with a keen eye, and I couldn't help but remember what Laura said that he was saying about me. "Out doing the shopping, are you, Carolyn?"

I looked up at him. "Why yes, I am."

He seemed to almost snicker, but then quickly hid it. "Did you forget to tie up your horse?"

I crossed my arms. "No, I am waiting for Jesse. He and Laura went somewhere and they said that they would be right back."

A sad look crossed his face. "I'm afraid not. I just saw them leaving town. Jesse told me that he had to get back home immediately and asked me to take you back."

I studied him. First of all, Cole thought my horse ran away and secondly, Jesse would never ask Cole to take me home, especially when he had Laura with him. "You are only on a horse, hardly enough room for all my packages. Anyway, Jesse wouldn't do that."

"Are you sure about that?"

"Quite sure," I replied, moving over to a bench to sit.

He shrugged. "Suit yourself. I hope you brought some money along to stay the night." Then he was off, but I could almost hear a hint of laughter. What was that all about? Jesse wasn't here yet, but it hadn't yet been twenty minutes.

Someone else rode up, but it wasn't Jesse or Cole. It

was Scott. He also pulled up on his horse, but instead of staying up there, he jumped down. "Did you see Cole Brown? I passed him coming here, and he was laughing so hard he almost fell off his horse."

I knew that Cole played a joke on me. "Yes, I saw him."

He looked off in the direction of town and then back at me. "Is Jesse here? I wanted to ask him something."

I nodded, "Yes, in fact, he should be here soon. He told me he would pick me up in twenty minutes and it is about that time now."

He grinned, "Good, I'll just wait here then." He sat down on the bench with me, but we didn't talk much. I had to keep telling myself that he was waiting here because of Jesse, not me!

Pretty soon, Jesse appeared, and he and Scott talked for a little, while Laura helped me load up the wagon. Soon, we were on our way. After we left town, Jesse handed me a letter, which was from *Mormor*. I eagerly read it and it was full of much news. Too much news to copy into here, but she says that she is well and that everything is going good in Sweden. I always treasure all my letters from Sweden. Back in my room, I have a little box under my bed filled with letters.

Sometimes, I'll go through them and re-read them.

November 13, 1854

Dear Diary,

Reverend Mast preached today on how we are to be a light to the world. Our love for Jesus should shine and everyone should be able to see it. Matthew 5:14-16 says, *"You are the light of the world. A city set on a hill cannot be hidden. Nor do people light a lamp and put it under a basket, but on a stand, and it gives light to all in the house. In the same way, let your light shine before others, so that they may see your good works and give glory to your Father who is in heaven."*

November 16, 1854

Dear Diary,

These past few days have been quite gloomy for us. Today would've been Momma's birthday, and knowing that it was coming and there was nothing to celebrate, it was hard. After Jesse, Bethy, and Laura trudged off to school, I saw Poppa going to Momma's grave with some stray wildflowers he had found. Knowing that no one was in the house, I went to Momma's trunk and pulled out one of her quilts. It still

smelled like her. I held her quilt close to me and cried into it.
Later, once I had finished crying, I went upstairs to read a bit
of Momma's diary like I have almost every night since I found
it. Somehow, in spite of the sadness that is hanging around
this day, it helped to read what Momma was thinking when
she was only thirteen years old.

November 18, 1854

Dear Dairy,

It snowed a little today, but not enough to amount to
much. I did some mending and sewing. While I did, I
imagined Momma sitting right across from me. I could hear
her laugh and her humming as she rocked in the rocker, back
and forth. Tears began rolling down my cheeks.

Before I knew it, Bethy and Laura came home from
school. Laura went right into the kitchen, but Bethy stopped
at the sight of me. "Have you been crying, Carolyn?"

My hands went to my face to wipe my tears and I
gave her a smile. "It's all right, dearest. I'm okay." She seemed
to accept that answer and went to go get her afternoon snack
with Laura.

November 19, 1854

Dear Diary,

Being that today was Saturday, I took Laura with me down to the cellar to help me count how many preserves we had left. We should have plenty, but in November, Momma always liked to count just to make sure we wouldn't run out, especially with the holidays and snowstorms coming. As expected, we were right on track.

After lunch, Bethy and I did a thorough cleaning of the house. At the end of the day, we did some more mending. It was a very productive day.

November 20, 1854

Dear Diary,

This morning, Reverend Mast compared last week's sermon to today's. This morning, he read from John 8:12. It says, *"Again Jesus spoke to them, saying, 'I am the light of the world. Whoever follows me will not walk in darkness, but will have the light of life.'"* Reverend Mast said that although we are to be lights and shine for Jesus, Jesus is also a light. He will guide us and we will never have to walk in darkness anymore. What an amazing thing that is!

November 21, 1854

Dear Diary,

I decided to rest today and write some more in my book. It is almost completed and I can't believe how fast the time has gone! I can't believe I only started writing this book in June.

The next segment is about the harvest. Summer and school have come to a close, and now it was time for us to harvest our crop that we had planted in the spring. We had already been planning to help Uncle Levi with his crop and the same with us, but what we hadn't been planning on was all the other neighbors and friends we had met who would help us out. In Sweden, every man was on his own, unless of course, family would pitch in. Here, everyone helps one another out. Mr. and Mrs. Holbrook and their family came, as well as the Bows. A couple other families came as well, but I can't quite remember their names. It was certainly a time for being thankful. Since Thanksgiving is almost upon us now, I can't help looking back to that time and thanking God that we were able to have such a wonderful start in our new life. We had brought in a bountiful crop that year, probably one of the best ones ever. It was truly a wonderful time.

November 23, 1854

Dear Diary,

I did some baking today, making a coconut mint pie and some rolls to bring to Aunt Maria's house for Thanksgiving dinner tomorrow. Since I knew tomorrow would be a busy day, I did some meditating today. I thought about all that I was thankful for. I am certainly thankful for my family and friends and even for a new life in America even though I miss Sweden. I'm not glad that God took Momma away, but I am thankful that he has helped my grief to slowly disappear. Yes, I miss her greatly and I wish she were here ever so much, but I know she is much happier in Heaven, and that helps to minimize my grieving. I am also very much thankful for all Momma has taught me about the housework. If she hadn't, we wouldn't be doing near as well as we are now. It is almost like she knew this would happen, and she wanted to make sure her family would be taken care of when she was gone. "We're doing okay, Momma," I whispered aloud. "We're doing okay." Then, this peace settled over me, and I knew that she heard me.

November 24, 1854

Dear Diary,

Thanksgiving Day is one of my most favorite days out of the year. For lunch, we headed over to Aunt Maria and Uncle Levi's place. I brought along my rolls, pie, and carrot casserole that I had just made this morning. Supper was very good, and we were all happy, and very thankful at how God brought us through the hard times of our lives.

November 26, 1854

Dear Diary,

Jesse rode into town today and when he got back, he delivered a letter to me from Millie. I went upstairs to read it right away. It said:

My dearest Carolyn,

How are you? It is beginning to get so cold here in Sweden, and now I remember why I don't like Sweden. It gets far too cold here in the winter. I suppose you are keeping busy, as am I. George and Phoebe are still not engaged, though I don't know what is taking so long. I try to drop hints, to both of them, if I have a good chance.

The other day when I was in the kitchen, George asked me if

I could make some of his favorite raisin nut cookies. I told him very sweetly, but tartly, "Find your own cook." He blushed and quickly left the kitchen. Then the next day when Phoebe was here, she asked me what his favorite cookies were. It took all the self-control I had in me not to sigh aloud. I told her that his favorite was raisin nut, but they had to be made with exactly twelve raisins in each. Her eyes got really big, but then I reassured her that I'm sure he wouldn't mind the number if they were made by her. Then she blushed and left. I do have the habit of making people leave me! But you won't believe it, the next day, Phoebe brought over a plate cookies, each with twelve raisins! That is when I left the room.

But enough about George and Phoebe, on to your problems that I have answers to! I can't believe that Sherry would say such horrid things about you! And Cole pretends to be nice to you? I don't have an answer about that, but in regards to Sherry. I say approach her. Tell her that you don't appreciate what she is saying, and tell her that you would much rather be in school (right?). Or, say that if she would rather take your place cooking, cleaning, and mending, go right ahead!

But that is just my opinion. Thankfully, there are no bullies around here at the present. But you never know. Sometimes, they just pop out!

I had better get going. Momma is calling, and I think she

figured out about what I told Phoebe about the cookies!

    Your dearest cousin,

    Millie

    Millie's letter brought on a strong desire of wanting to see her. How I wish I could've seen her when she was meddling with her brother's girlfriend. I do hope Aunt Melissa won't be too angry with her, for I'm sure Phoebe wasn't. And I don't think I will follow her ideas about Sherry. Millie is a bit more outgoing than me, and I don't think I would have the courage to say those things to her face! Oh well, Momma would say to just ignore it and wear a smile.

November 27, 1854

Dear Diary,

    Reverend Mast preached today on David's song of thanks which is in 1 Chronicles chapter 16, verses 8-36. Verse 8 says, *"Oh give thanks to the Lord; call upon his name; make known his deeds among the people."* The rest of the song talks about all of God's greatness and all He has done and how we are to praise Him. David went through many trials and temptations in his life, but through it all, he praised God. And that is what we are to do. We are to praise whatever that circumstance may be; no matter what we are going through.

"Blessed be the Lord, the God of Israel, from everlasting to everlasting!"

November 28, 1854

Dear Diary,

Mrs. Miller stopped by and said she wanted to speak with Poppa. I told her he was out in the barn, and I wish I would've thought more before I answered. What could Mrs. Miller possibly want with my Poppa? She had better not want to marry him, for Poppa would never betray Momma in that way. Not this soon. Nevertheless, I am going to keep my eye on her.

December 1, 1854

Dear Diary,

It is a rainy day today, not quite snow, almost like sleet. I decided to take advantage of the dreariness and write some more in my book. It is almost complete, and I am trying to finish it in time for Christmas.

The next part is about Thanksgiving. Our first Thanksgiving in America we were invited to the Holbrook's as well as Uncle Levi's family. It was wonderful to be surrounded by family and old friends.

As you could probably tell, we were close with the Holbrooks. They left about a year ago for California. Their oldest son Caleb had left two years ago in search for gold, and he found some. Mr. and Mrs. Holbrook decided to join him, as well as their younger son Daniel, who is Jesse's age, and younger daughter Marie, who was one of my good friends. We haven't heard from them at all. But writing now about how welcomed they made us feel here, makes me want to write them and tell them what has been happening. Momma and Mrs. Holbrook were good friends, and I'm sure she would like to know about her death. Though I'm not sure how I would reach them. California is a pretty big state and the Holbrooks are a small family.

Season 3

December 2, 1854

Dear Diary,

I am now turning my focus upon the upcoming Christmas season, which is speedily approaching. I am so excited to begin all our Christmas traditions. Tomorrow, Poppa has said that we can go to pick and cut down our Christmas tree. Our very first tradition, but I shall explain them all as they approach!

Christmas will be different this year without Momma. She loved Christmas, it was her favorite season. I am going to do my very best to do everything like she would've. Even though Momma is not here, our traditions will survive and new memories will be born.

December 3, 1854

Dear Diary,

After a hearty breakfast of eggs and bacon, we bundled up and set off to the woods in the wagon. Sometimes we take the sleigh, but you can't drive a sleigh if there is no snow. Picking out a tree is a very difficult task. It must be perfect--perfect height, perfect width, and perfect color--if it is not, we move on to the next tree. When we come upon our tree, everyone feels it. You just get this warm feeling inside and you know! Finally we found our tree, and it was perfect. Poppa and Jesse took turns swinging the ax to cut it down and soon it was loaded into the wagon.

When we got home, I made hot chocolate for everyone and then the girls and I started making lunch. After lunch, Poppa and Jesse brought the tree in, which is a task in itself, while Bethy, Laura, and I made popcorn garlands. Then we decorated the tree and the girls and I broke out in Christmas songs. It was a good day, and I knew Momma was smiling down on us, singing along.

December 4, 1854

Dear Diary,

To begin the Christmas season, Reverend Mast started preparing us for Jesus' birth by beginning with his mother, Mary. Mary was a young girl chosen by God to be his Son's mother. Mary, even though she was young, trusted God. Luke 1:38 says, *"And Mary said, 'Behold, I am the servant of the Lord; let it be to me according to your word.'"*

Then Mary visited her cousin Elizabeth, and Mary praised the Lord. Luke 1:46-47 says, *"And Mary said, 'My soul magnifies the Lord, and my spirit rejoices in God my Savior.'"* I'd like to think that if I had been in Mary's position, I would have done the same thing. Even though this virgin pregnancy would bring scandal for herself and her family, Mary wasn't afraid. She was ready and able to do as the Lord had commanded her to do.

December 6, 1854

Dear Diary,

I rode over to Aunt Maria's this morning. I wanted to ask her if by any chance she had the Holbrook's address. She said that she did not, but if I brought a letter to the post office, they might know. Before I left, I asked her about one more thing. "Do you think Poppa is considering marriage to Mrs. Miller?"

Aunt Maria continued her sewing, "Now, Carolyn, I'm not one to meddle, but I think your Poppa does admire Mrs. Miller. I wouldn't go as far to say that he is going to marry her yet, but it might come in time."

I collapsed back on the chair. "But, Aunt Maria, how can Poppa even consider something like that so soon after Momma's death? How could he betray her?"

Aunt Maria looked up at me, and took my hands in hers. "My dear, no one can replace your mother and it would not be betraying her. Your Poppa loved her so much, and she him. She would want him to be happy and love again. Your mother will always be in his heart, as she will always be in yours, but that doesn't mean there can't be another. And, I believe he is doing it for you and your sisters. He thinks you girls need to have a mother to continue teaching you, and so you don't carry everything on your own."

I tried to hold back my tears. "But what if I'm not ready for another mother?"

Aunt Maria pulled me into her arms. "It will take time, and I don't think it will happen for quite a while yet. Don't worry about it now. Pray about it."

I knew she was right, and the whole ride home, I asked God to give me peace if it was his plan for us to have another mother.

December 7, 1854

Dear Diary,

I did some more decorating today, placing garlands and candles around the house just as Momma had. I wanted this Christmas to be special and not crowded with the unwanted feelings I had yesterday, so I tried to push it all out of my head. Later in the day, I did some baking and made a couple loaves of bread and also some beef stew for supper tonight. When the day was through, the house looked like Christmas and even smelled a little like it too!

December 8, 1854

Dear Diary,

When Jesse and the girls got home from school today, Jesse handed me an invitation. While I opened it, he cautioned me saying, "Please don't go crazy. It could be fun." I opened it, and this is what is said:

Mr. Cole and Miss Sherry Brown

Invite

Mr. Jesse and Miss Carolyn Woodsmall

To their Christmas Ball

December 26 at 5pm

I wasn't quite sure what to think. Me, the girl who was bullied by Sherry, invited to a ball at the Brown's? It seemed like quite a contradiction to me. When I looked up from the invitation, Jesse and the girls were looking at me expectantly. I looked at each of them, "What?" I could tell Jesse seemed nervous.

"What do you think?"

I tucked the invitation back into the envelope. "I'm not sure what to think."

Laura took the invitation out of my hand, pulled it out, and scanned it over. "Are you going to go?"

I turned to the kitchen. "Why not? It is a ball." And

that was the end of that. We were going, and why shouldn't we? I'm lucky I was invited at all since I don't go to school anymore. But then again, maybe her mother forced her to invite us Woodsmalls. I mentally scolded myself; I shouldn't be thinking bad thoughts about them since they had invited us.

Jesse and I told Poppa the news at supper, and he seemed pleased for us. "A new tradition for you, Carrie," he said warmly. Yes, indeed, a very new one.

December 9, 1854

Dear Diary,

Kirsten came over from school and asked if I would be going to the ball. I told her that I was and she was so happy. "Even though I don't like the Browns very much, I'm not going to turn down a party!" she said very excitedly. "Oh and Momma said tomorrow she is going to take us shopping for our dress material, as long as you are not busy."

I laughed, "Me, busy? I am free the whole day!" Kirsten gave me a hug, and we laughed excitedly together.

December 10, 1854

Dear Diary,

Aunt Maria and Kirsten came by in the morning and after leaving Bethy instructions on what to make for lunch, we were soon on our way. It was so much fun to actually go shopping for satin and trimmings. I'm not sure if I ever owned a fancy dress before. Once we finally made up our minds, Kirsten settled with a dark blue satin with white lace trimming and I had dark red with trimming. Aunt Maria remarked that we would be the loveliest girls in all of Minnesota. I'm not sure if that is actually true, but it is fun to imagine!

December 11, 1854

Dear Diary,

As we move through the Christmas story, we come to Joseph. Reverend Mast talked about how Joseph was in the line of King David and he was a poor carpenter, engaged to Mary. But, when he found out that Mary was pregnant, he was full of doubts and thoughts of betrayal. But an angel came to him and told him to marry Mary anyway, for her child was God's son. So Joseph did, even though it went against everything he had been taught; even though his family and customers might ridicule him and not believe Joseph was telling the truth. But Joseph decided to trust God anyway. Matthew 1: 21 says, *"She will bear a son, and you shall call his name Jesus, for he will save the people from their sins."*

December 12, 1854

Dear Diary,

It has begun snowing a bit today and I am desperately hoping that it will continue so that we may have a white Christmas. Christmas Eve sleigh rides are my absolute favorite!

This afternoon, I did some sewing for I need to finish Poppa and Jesse's winter coats for their Christmas presents. They are pretty much done, but just a few more stiches need to be added. Then I need to finish a quilt for Bethany, a dress for Laura, shawls for Kirsten and Aunt Maria, as well as scarves for Luke and Uncle Levi. Quite a lot to do yet, but I still have almost two weeks till Christmas.

December 13, 1854

Dear Diary,

Today is St. Lucia's Day. Every year on this day, I dress up as St. Lucia and bring coffee and buns around to my family in the morning. This is a tradition that we celebrated in Sweden, but we still like to do it in America. St. Lucia was a girl long ago who was martyred for her faith. She would wear candles on her head and bring food to Christians who were hiding from Roman soldiers to keep from being persecuted themselves. Now, girls celebrate by wearing a crown of candles on their head and a white dress with a red sash. The oldest daughter plays St. Lucia and she brings around breakfast to her family. I do believe that this is my favorite Christmas tradition.

December 15, 1854

Dear Diary,

Five years ago today, we arrived in America from Sweden. It is hard to believe that it has been that long already. As I was remembering the day, I wrote some more in my book and actually finished it!

This last segment is about our second Christmas. Our

first Christmas was a bit rushed and we didn't celebrate much, but this second year, Poppa had money from our crop and he bought us all presents and a wonderful dinner. Uncle Levi, Aunt Maria, Herb, Luke, and Kirsten came over and as we crammed in our small cabin, we read the Christmas story, ate a wonderful meal, opened presents, and realized how fortunate we were to be together. Poppa even announced that next spring he was going to build us a house. I could see tears in Momma's eyes and I knew then that she was so happy. We all were. It was one of the best Christmases ever.

December 17, 1854

Dear Diary,

I began working on my ball dress today. Why must I always procrastinate?! Bethy offered to help me, so while she worked on the bodice, I did the skirt. Caddie and Julie came by later in the day wondering if they could play with Laura and Bethy, so I let Bethy go and soon I was working on the dress by myself.

I must have lost track of time, for the next thing I knew, Jesse was walking through the door. "Laura wanted me to ask you if Caddie and Julie can stay for supper."

I shrugged, "Fine with me."

He was about to leave, then he paused. "What is for supper?"

I jerked my head up and looked to the kitchen. My fire had gone low and nothing was ready, "Is it time now?"

Jesse slowly nodded his head. I gently put away my dress. "I'll go get something ready." I dashed off to the kitchen and I could hear Jesse's laughter as he walked out the door.

Luckily, I had some leftover chicken soup from last night, and only Jesse knew how flustered I really was. That evening, Bethy and I worked more on my gown. It was shaping out nicely and I have no doubt that it will be finished in time.

December 18, 1854

Dear Diary,

The next part of our Christmas story was about Joseph and Mary traveling to Bethlehem. Reverend Mast said that they had to go to Bethlehem because Joseph was from there and all people from Bethlehem must be counted. When they got to the home of a relative, there was no room in the inn, so they went outside to sleep in the stable. There, Jesus, the Son of God, was born. *Luke 2:7 says, "And she gave birth to her firstborn son and wrapped him in swaddling cloths and laid him in a manger, because there was no place for them in the inn."*

December 19, 1854

Dear Diary,

Since the girls and Jesse are off from school for the Christmas holiday, I enlisted Bethy to finish my dress while Laura helped me with the wash. Since it was so cold outside, we washed our clothes in the kitchen. It was nice and warm in there, so the clothes dried quickly.

By evening, Bethy had my dress pretty well complete. I tried it on and it fit perfectly! All she had to do was the hem. I couldn't wait to wear it for the ball!

December 20, 1854

Dear Diary,

It started snowing a little today, but I had Jesse ride into town to mail a letter to the Holbrooks for me as well as check the mail. Bethy and Laura also went out to the barn to play with their dolls, so I was able to work on everyone's Christmas presents. By lunch, I had finished Jesse, Poppa,

Bethy, and Laura's presents. It's good I did, for everyone seemed to be home then. Jesse said that the postman figured he could hopefully locate the Holbrooks, but I shouldn't get my hopes up. I tried not to, but I think they were already up.

December 21, 1854

Dear Diary,

The girls and I made Swedish maple cookies and cinnamon raisin buns this morning. These will be for Christmas Eve supper and Momma made them every year. Christmas Eve night, we go over to Aunt Maria's and have a big supper and open presents. Then on Christmas morning, everyone goes to church for a Christmas service and that evening the children go caroling to all the farmhouses in the area. How I love this season.

December 22, 1854

Dear Diary,

It snowed some more today and I am getting excited. I love when it snows at Christmastime. As long as we don't have a blizzard, we can take the sleigh to the ball!

December 23, 1854

Dear Diary,

I finished all of my Christmas presents; talk about cutting it close. As I was working in the kitchen today, I imagined Momma standing there. She didn't say anything, just watched me as I made eggnog, bread, and soup. At one time, I thought she might've been an angel, but when I reached out to touch her, she was gone. I told myself that I was seeing things, so I left the room to set the table for supper.

December 24, 1854

Dear Diary,

It is finally Christmas Eve! This morning, I made a pumpkin pie and rolls to bring over to Aunt Maria's. Then the girls and I sat around the tree in the afternoon and sewed and talked. It was nice just to sit inside with a roaring fire and a house the smelled like Christmas. Bethy had remarked that she wished Momma were here. I told her that Momma is here, in our hearts and our minds.

Around five, we headed over to Aunt Maria's house. After eating a delicious supper, Poppa and Uncle Levi read the Christmas story. Even though I have heard the story many times growing up, I never get tired of hearing it. I am just in awe of the wonderful things God can do, even to a couple so poor. They got to raise the Son of God as their own child!

I got many wonderful presents, such as a new hat, a journal to write my stories in, a quilt rack, a woolen bonnet, and a lacy shawl to go with my dress for the ball. In addition to all the gifts I gave, there was one more gift for the whole family. It was the book about our journey from Sweden to America. I read it to everyone, and I think everyone was crying by the end. Aunt Maria said it was a way for us to remember how much we have been through, and Poppa said that I will make a very fine *forfattare* when I grow up. Then, we all got into the sleigh, and went home and thus ended Christmas Eve.

December 25, 1854

Dear Diary,

God Jul! Merry Christmas! We all woke up bright and early, and I made an egg and sausage bake for breakfast. Then, we all dressed in our church outfits and rode to church.

Reverend Mast's Christmas message was on the shepherds
and how they received the good news of Jesus' birth. It is
hard for me to imagine what I would've done if I was a
shepherd, watching my sheep. I think if a very bright light
appeared and started talking to me I would've been terrified.
I would have run as far as I could away from the pastures and
got Poppa! But the shepherds didn't. Instead, they listened to
what the angel had said and they did it. Luke 2:14 says,
*"Glory to God in the highest, and on earth peace among those with
whom he is pleased."*

Reverend Mast touched on Mary's feelings. Here she
was, a young girl in a stable, and those dirty shepherds came
in and worshiped her baby. Then, this little baby was being
praised and the shepherds were glorifying God and giving
him all the praise. Luke 2:19 says, *"But Mary treasured up all
these things, pondering them in her heart."* She held everything
close and she thought about it. She must've thought about the
angel she saw and how everything came true just like he said.
She must've been thinking way back in the books of the
prophets and how the things they had foretold and the
Messiah were coming true. And she was the mother of this
Son of God. What an amazing feeling that must've been.
Something we can't even begin to imagine.

December 27, 1854

Dear Diary,

Yesterday evening, Jesse and I attended the Browns' Christmas ball. It was such a wonderful evening, well most of it, and I have so much to write.

As we were preparing to go, I dressed in my dark red ball dress with the lacy trimming and my lacy shawl that Kirsten gave me. Bethy also put my hair in curls that lay beautifully down my back. When I came down the stairs, Poppa said I looked just like Momma when she was thirteen. Hearing him say that put a smile on my face, but also longing in my soul. How I wish that Momma could see me going to my first ball. Then, I put on my big woolen shawl and bonnet and hurried outside to where Jesse had the sleigh ready. We picked up Kirsten and Luke first, and then drove over to the Brown's house.

The house looked stunning and there were lanterns all around the walkway to the house, which looked lovely with the snow that was falling ever so gently. There was such an abundance of food, and I must say, Mrs. Brown, and I suppose Sherry too, did a wonderful job preparing it.

There was lots of music and dancing, and I believe I

danced my fill when the evening finally ended. I danced with Jesse, Luke, Scott Harp, Herbert Bow, Hank Bow, and even Cole Brown. I was actually surprised when he (Cole) asked me to dance. It wasn't all that bad, but he didn't talk much to me, just about himself and I found him rather self-centered. On the other hand, dancing with Scott was wonderful. He said that Jesse told him about the book I had written and he was wondering if he could read it sometime. I said that I didn't know why he couldn't!

I must say though, I was quite disappointed when we had to leave. Luke came over to Kirsten and me around midnight and said that Jesse had just gone out to get the sleigh. It was starting to snow harder and pile up, and Jesse and Luke wanted to get home before it got too bad. Unfortunately, we were not even half way home before the lightly falling snow turned into a real blizzard. I was glad that I was in the back of the sleigh wrapped under warm blankets with Kirsten and not up on the driver's seat with Jesse and Luke.

Pretty soon, we couldn't even see what was right in front of us, and I could tell that the horse was uneasy, because he kept starting and stopping. Jesse got down to lead the horse. "Don't worry, we'll be home soon!" he yelled to us girls seated in the back. I couldn't help but worry. Here we were, and I didn't even know where, with a blizzard roaring around us. Jesse was out walking in front of the horse and I couldn't see him anymore. Luke yelled back to Kirsten and I not to go to sleep, and we tried very hard not to. My eyes just wanted to close, but I knew it was likely we would freeze to death if we did fall asleep.

Suddenly, we jerked to a stop. My first thought was that the horse was too scared to move. My second was we had hit a fence, but who's? Could it possibly be ours or Uncle Levi's? But when we didn't start up again, I began getting worried. I stood up to ask Luke what was wrong, and he handed me the reins while he got down to find Jesse. Kirsten and I waited, but neither Luke nor Jesse came back. I couldn't wait any longer and I was about to go look for myself, when Luke was suddenly next to us with Jesse leaning heavily on Luke's side. I think I screamed even though I couldn't hear it, and I jumped down next to him. He was hurt bad, twisted ankle, I thought, and possibly a broken foot. He had tripped on a rock and that rock had a jagged point. Together, Luke and I got Jesse up on the sleigh, and Kirsten got a place ready for him in the back. I tried to get Jesse comfortable and wake him up, but he wasn't stirring. "We have to get home!" I told

Luke. "Jesse's not stirring."

We started moving again, with Luke leading the horse, Kirsten at the reins, and me at my brother's side. I checked Jesse's feet to make sure they weren't frostbitten and when I saw they weren't, I began rubbing them furiously, trying to warm them. Nevertheless, he didn't wake and when I looked up, we had not moved at all, everything was the same. "Oh, God, please help us! Help us find shelter!" I prayed aloud. I knew God would hear me. He has heard my cries very much of late and surely he would still answer now. Almost instantly, we came to a sudden stop. Kirsten and I jerked up, aware of what happened last time this happened. I was about to get out, but we started moving again. Perhaps we ran into a fence and Luke was following it? Oh, I prayed it was so!

It was! Not long after our stop, we came upon a building and it was Aunt Maria's and Uncle Levi's. How relieved we were to see them and they to see us! We hurried inside and warmed up by the fire. Jesse awoke and we all took the much longed for rest that we needed.

Sometime after breakfast that morning, the storm stopped and Uncle Levi took Jesse and I home. Poppa, Bethy, and Laura were so relieved to see that we were all right.

Poppa had said that he was just getting ready to take off for Uncle Levi's place to see if we were there.

Now we are all home safe and sound, and I believe that I am going to catch up on my long needed rest!

December 28, 1854

Dear Diary,

I slept most of the morning, but when I did come down, it was nice to find Bethy making lunch. Laura was doing some mending and Poppa was out in the barn. Jesse was upstairs in bed resting, since he had indeed twisted his ankle and there was a nasty cut that traveled the length of his lower leg. It looks like it would be very painful, but Jesse doesn't complain at all.

December 29, 1854

Dear Diary,

There is so much snow on the ground, Poppa says about four feet. Bethy and I looked over my dress this afternoon, and I was relieved that it is not damaged very much. There are a couple tears but other than being wet, it is fine.

December 30, 1854

Dear Diary,

Laura and I made raspberry nut cookies this morning and Bethy did some mending. Jesse's foot is doing a little better, but I believe he will be stuck in bed for a week or so yet. He is not quite happy about that news. I am slowly settling back into my routine, but part of me would like to have parties like that all the time. It was truly a wonderful time.

December 31, 1854

Dear Diary,

I can hardly believe that it is already New Year's Eve. Usually, Uncle Levi, Aunt Maria, Luke, and Kirsten come here, but they have decided to stay home this year because of the snow. So Poppa, the girls, and I all celebrated the end of 1854 together. It was a pretty small occasion. I made beef stew and we sat around the fire. Poppa even told some stories about when he was a boy growing up in Sweden. This was something new for me. Poppa never used to tell stories, but that's because Momma always did. Perhaps he is trying to fill that void, and it certainly cheered the girls and me up.

January 1, 1855

Dear Diary,

God *fortsattning*! Happy New Year! I can hardly believe that it is really the New Year. After everything that I have been through this last year, I am anxious about what this year may bring.

Reverend Mast spoke on how we must dedicate this New Year to God. Proverbs 3:5-6 says, *"Trust in the Lord with all your heart, and do not lean on your own understanding. In all your ways acknowledge him, and he will make straight your paths."* I have determined to myself that I will trust God even more than I have the previous year. How wonderful a feeling to know that God will take care of me and all I have to do is trust him.

January 2, 1855

Dear Diary,

I spent today in the kitchen, making bread, chicken soup, and also *pepparkokor* (gingerbread). Poppa loves gingerbread. Bethy and Laura were playing outside and Jesse was still confined to his bed. I could tell he was getting quite bored, but then Scott Harp and his sisters came by. Caddie

and Julie went to play with Bethy and Laura, and Scott came
up to see Jesse. Jesse was no doubt thrilled to see the face of
someone other than his sisters, so I let the two boys be.

January 3, 1855

Dear Diary,

The girls went back to school today. The house was
ever so much quieter than it was yesterday. Poppa was
outside, no doubt chopping wood, even though everything
was still covered by snow. I changed Jesse's wraps today and
the cut was looking a lot better.

January 4, 1855

Dear Diary,

I made *kanel* buns (cinnamon buns) this morning,
which are Jesse's favorite. When I brought them up, he was so
excited to see them. I stayed up there a little bit while Jesse
ate, for in truth I was getting a bit lonely downstairs and it is
nice to have some company. We talked about the ball for a
little, and apparently he enjoyed it as much as I did.

January 5, 1855

Dear Diary,

I did some cleaning today. My! The house was indeed quite dirty. It seems that it is not at all possible to try and take a week off now and again, especially in the winter time. Jesse's foot is doing much better, and I do believe that he will be able to go back to school soon, Monday at the earliest. When I told him, he almost jumped out of bed for he was so excited. I scolded him very gently. "Now, Jesse, if you re-hurt your foot from your excitement, you'll be in bed for another week." That settled him down very quickly!

January 6, 1855

Dear Diary,

When I brought lunch up to Jesse today, he continued talking to me and I wasn't able to go back down for my own lunch. Apparently, he was still thinking about the ball. Then suddenly, he told me, "You know, Carrie, Cole Brown and Scott both told me that they really like you."

I recoiled in shock. "Well, I don't like him one bit!"

I was about to leave, when Jesse remarked, "You said 'him' which is singular, so now I know you like one of them."

I left the room before Jesse could get any more secret information out of me.

January 7, 1855

Dear Diary,

Since the girls were home today, I decided to do the wash. There was still snow on the ground, so unfortunately we couldn't do it outside, but we did do it in the kitchen.

Jesse is slowly walking around, so he will probably go to school on Monday. I must say, I do believe I have gotten used to him being around and therefore will miss him when he goes. But I shall get on like I normally do. Maybe I shall start another book; that kept my days busy before.

January 9, 1855

Dear Diary,

Bethy and Laura brought their skates to school with them, because at recess the school children were going to go ice skating. Even though Jesse was able to go to school today, Poppa told him not to bring his, because his foot just healed. Then Poppa went hunting after Jesse and the girls left for school, and he said he wouldn't be back till tomorrow at lunchtime.

I was anticipating a nice restful day at home, even if no one was around. I baked this morning, and after lunch, I settled down to get some sewing done. I have almost finished the blanket that I was making, and I wanted to get it finished before another snowstorm hit. I didn't get much accomplished though, for the next thing I knew there was a pounding on the door. I opened it, and there was Kirsten, panting for breath "Jesse fell in the lake. You're supposed to bring the sleigh."

I grabbed my shawl and hurried out after Kirsten, hitching the sleigh up as quickly as I could. On our way there, Kirsten told me that apparently Jesse brought his skates to school and hurt his foot again, fell, and broke the ice. Luke told her to run and get a sleigh, and when she left, Scott and Luke were just pulling him out.

When we got there, Jesse was lying on the snow, apparently unconscious, and Bethy was kneeling at his side. Luke and Scott placed Jesse in the sleigh, and Laura and Bethy climbed in beside him. Luke offered to come with us, but I told him we'd be fine.

I got Jesse home and put him on the couch. Bethy heated up some stew and Laura found some more blankets. I gently inspected his foot and noted that it wasn't as bad as I had thought. His wound wasn't reopened, but he might've sprained it again. It was pretty late, when he finally aroused. I scolded him as gently as I could, "Jesse, how could've you gone on the ice. Poppa told you not to."

Jesse gave me a weak smile. "Ahh, Carrie, you would've gone too." He settled back on the pillows and fell asleep again.

January 10, 1855

Dear Diary,

I woke up this morning with a kink in my neck because I slept on a chair next to Jesse. Surprisingly enough, he was able to walk around this morning and pleaded with me to let him go to school. Of course, I said no, but then Jesse went anyway because he argued that he was older than me. So, Jesse and the girls left for school and I stayed home.

Around lunchtime, I set a place for Poppa at the table, but he didn't come. It didn't worry me too much, for I just assumed that the snow had given him a setback. When the girls walked in the house after school, I started to worry. Poppa should've been home by now, but he wasn't. After

supper, it was getting dark, so Jesse went out to look for him.
The girls and I waited back home. We tried to sew, but I
seemed to be messing up more than making any progress.

It was almost midnight, so I sent the girls up to bed.
They didn't want to go, but with school tomorrow, I insisted.
Not long after that, the door flew open and Jesse entered,
half-carrying, half-dragging Poppa behind him. Poppa's shirt
was caked in blood, and Jesse told me that he was clawed by
a bear. I settled him on the floor of the kitchen where it was
warm, and began peeling off his shirt. The sight of all that
blood made my stomach lurch. He was bleeding very heavily,
and for a second I couldn't move. I didn't know what to do. I
heard the door open and shut, but I didn't know what Jesse
was planning on doing. Finally, I stood up and got some
water and alcohol to begin cleaning his wounds. When I
would place the rag on his wound, he seemed to wince a
little, but his eyes remained closed.

Jesse came back inside and knelt beside me. "Listen,
Carrie, I'm going to take Poppa to the doctor."

I nodded. "That would be wise. There is so much
blood, and I don't know what to do."

He squeezed my shoulder. "Don't worry, he'll be okay.
I might have to stay in town for a little bit, or at least for

tomorrow, so don't stray too much from home."

I could see worry in his face. I wasn't sure if that was for Poppa or leaving us girls home alone. "Okay, I won't go anywhere."

"Keep the girls here too."

I nodded again. "Okay. I promise."

We got Poppa loaded in the sleigh and then they left. I went back inside and latched the door behind me. I couldn't help but feel a little frightened being left home alone in the night.

January 11, 1855

Dear Diary,

I kept the girls home from school today and we tried to keep as busy as we could. Around mid-morning, Laura and I went out to do the barn chores and as we were coming back in, it was starting to snow. After that, I worked in the kitchen a bit, making some beef stew and bread while Bethy and Laura were doing some mending.

About supper time, Laura and I went back out to do the nighttime chores so we wouldn't have to go out when it was dark. As Laura was finishing up, I was starting to take loads of wood into the house. I was on one of these trips, when a horse and rider appeared. It was Luke. When he saw me, he quickly got off of his horse. "Momma wanted me to check on your family, since the girls and Jesse weren't at school today."

"Well, last night, Poppa was clawed by a bear when he was hunting, so Jesse took him to town. He wanted me to keep the girls here too."

Luke took the wood from my arms and walked it to the house. "If you want, I'm sure you can come and stay with us."

I shook my head as we walked up the steps. "No, we'll be okay. They'll be back tomorrow, I'm sure. And it would be nice to keep a fire warm for them."

Luke just sighed as he put his stack of wood down on the pile at the one end of the porch, "If you say so, Carolyn."

That night, I dreadfully wished Poppa and Jesse were here or else we had gone to Aunt Maria's. It's kind of eerie sleeping in a house with only your younger sisters. After I put the girls to bed, I stayed up, just listening to every little sound and wondering what it was. I tried to reassure myself that Jesse would've never left us here by ourselves if it wasn't safe. Nevertheless, I made sure the door was latched securely.

January 12, 1855

Dear Diary,

Around lunchtime, it started snowing pretty hard and around supper when I went out to do the barn chores, it was turning into a real blizzard. I kept Laura inside with Bethy when I went out, for I didn't need to worry about her. As I went, I took a rope with me that attached to the main house. I was quite relieved when I finally reached the barn door and pushed it open. It was warm in the barn, most likely from all

the animals. Still, it took me twice as long to do the chores since there was no one to help me.

As I was putting hay in the horses' feed trough, the door flew open. A tall figure stood in the doorway. I gave a small scream and grabbed the pitchfork, which was right next to me.

The figure came closer with his hands in the air. "Relax, Carolyn, it's only me." It was Scott Harp.

With a sigh of relief, I lowered my pitchfork, "You know, you shouldn't scare people like that."

He gave a small laugh. "I reckon not."

I continued my job at hand. "So, what are you doing here? I would have thought that Luke would've told you that Jesse wasn't here."

Scott started filling another trough with hay, "He did, but we both thought that it would be good for someone to check up on you girls."

I turned to him. "We don't need checking up on, and besides, with a blizzard, there is no need for anyone to put their lives at risk."

Scott stopped what he was doing and looked my way. "Then just let the barn alone and stay inside and I won't come anymore."

That was ridiculous. "I can't do that! They'll die out
here. What would Poppa and Jesse say when they return and
all their animals are dead?"

"They'll say that at least you and the girls were safe.
Just think if you were to get lost out here. How would the
girls find you?"

"My sentiments exactly, which is why I have a rope
hanging from the house to the barn. And you do not, so you
should get home before you get lost."

"Carolyn..."

"The blizzard might be over tomorrow anyway. There
is no sense in arguing this." I walked over to the door and
swung it open. There was nothing but absolute whiteness out
there. I couldn't even see the rope hanging in front of me. I
grabbed some pieces of wood before I grabbed to the rope
with one hand. I turned then to look at Scott who was just
standing there, watching me with a face that showed he
disapproved. I tried to smile, but none would come. "Please
shut the door when you leave." Then I left, out into the
whiteness all alone. The wind was so strong that I lost all of
my wood pieces, but I didn't stop for them. I could hold the
rope easier now with two hands, though it was swinging
rapidly back and forth.

Finally, I stumbled upon the steps. Crawling up, I pushed the door open and collapsed inside the house.

"Carolyn!" Bethy screamed upon my entrance. She and Laura pulled me in and settled me by the fire. It took me this long to get here, how would Scott possibly get home?

January 13, 1855

Dear Diary,

Well, the snow has not subsided and it seems to be getting worse and worse. I stayed inside today, but it was desperately hard not to go out and check on the animals. I tried to get Bethy and Laura to work on some schoolwork, but it is so hard to concentrate when you can hear the wind howling and moaning from outside.

January 14, 1855

Dear Diary,

I am beginning to worry about Poppa and Jesse. Where are they? I wish Jesse could send word to us, but nothing could possibly get through in this storm. I was going to go feed the animals today, but when I looked out the window, I couldn't even see the rope that was attached to the post. Perhaps tomorrow I shall go. Like Scott had said, what would the girls do if I didn't come back? And Jesse didn't specifically tell me to continue the barn chores, but then again, he thought he would've been back by now.

January 15, 1855

Dear Diary,

The days get even colder as the blizzard keeps going on and on. We sit mostly around the fire all day, sewing and studying, and we're even sleeping down in the living room, so it's easier to keep the fire going. Today, I read a scripture about not worrying about anything -- God will provide. Matthew 6:25 and 33 says, *"Therefore I tell you, do not be anxious about your life, what you will eat or what you will drink, nor about your body, what you will put on. Is not life more important than food, and the body more that clothing? But seek first the kingdom of God and his righteousness, and all these things will be added unto you."*

January 16, 1855

Dear Diary,

I decided that I must go out today for it has been a few

days since I fed the animals. After telling the girls to mind the fire and to not venture out of the house no matter what, I left. I don't even know how to describe it, but it was so white, I literally couldn't see what was right in front of me. Grasping on the rope, I took one step at a time, praying that I wouldn't stumble and lose hold of the rope. It seemed like forever, but I eventually made it to the barn. Our milk cow was mooing very loudly to be fed and milked, and the chickens and horses were making quite a ruckus too. I fed them, going as fast as I could so I could get back to the warmth of my house. After making sure I gave the animals a double feeding, I ventured out again into the bleak whiteness. Step by step, I inched my way along, praying that God would allow me to get safely home to my sisters. He did, and soon I was inside by the warm fire, drinking some hot tea.

January 17, 1855

Dear Diary,

The wind is still howling away and I am getting worried about what might happen to us. Our wood pile is rapidly depleting, since we are using wood all hours of the day. Our food supply is running low, but I suppose we have food in the cellar but I'm not sure I would be able to get inside since the door is probably covered with snow. I am terrified, but I try not to let the girls see my terror. I am anxious about Poppa and Jesse in town and how they are doing. I do so hope that they are not stuck in the prairie somewhere and freeze to death. But when we were sitting down this evening, Bethy found this verse in the Bible. Matthew 6:34 says, *"Therefore do not be anxious about tomorrow, for tomorrow will be anxious for itself. Sufficient for the day its own troubles."* God will provide all our needs and he will see us through this blizzard. If only I remember that.

January 18, 1855

Dear Diary,

I journeyed out to the barn this morning again. It seems like every time I go the snow drifts get higher and higher. After I fed the animals, I looked around the whole barn at what I could possibly use for kindling. I found a pile of scrap wood in the back, so as I trudged back, I carried as much of the wood that I could.

January 19, 1855

Dear Diary,

Since the wood pile is so low, I try to use the least possible amount of wood. In addition to the wood shortage, we are on the last of the soup. Only a few more days and we shall be drinking hot tea and eating crackers!

January 21, 1855

Dear Diary,

It is just as I had predicted--we are out of food. I can't even believe that it has come to this, for I thought we had plenty of food! How I pray that the wind would stop.

January 22, 1855

Dear Diary,

The wood pile is out. I told Bethy and Laura to stay in bed and not to move. I resorted to desperate measures and broke apart one of our chairs. It was so hard to do. I had no idea that those chairs were so sturdy. One piece at a time, I tossed our chair into the fire. I suppose that chair will last us for today and I am ready to tear apart the next chair for tomorrow.

January 23, 1855

Dear Diary,

It is freezing inside even though I put some more chairs into the fire. At one point during the day, I stood in front of the window just praying that it would stop. I knew that we would all die soon. Almost two days without nourishment and now I am breaking apart the furniture to burn. I could feel tears pooling in my eyes, but I did not want to cry in front of my sisters. Suddenly, Bethy started singing:

> *In the rifted rock I'm resting,*
> *Safely sheltered I abide;*
> *There no foes nor storms molest me,*
> *While within the cleft I hide.*

Laura had joined Bethy on the chorus, and it was the most beautiful sound I had heard in so long.

> *Now I'm resting, sweetly resting*
> *In the cleft once made for me;*
> *Jesus, Blessed Rock of Ages,*
> *I will hide myself in thee.*

The tears were flowing down my cheeks now in a steady stream. But even though I was worried about what might happen to us, we were sheltered in God's arms and he will protect us.

January 24, 1855

Dear Diary,

The wind has subsided! I can hardly believe it myself, but when I looked out the window, I could finally see a faint glimmer of sunlight. I put one last chair into the fire. We were going to be okay.

That afternoon, Bethy and Laura worked at folding our makeshift beds, and I went outside to check on the animals again. Surprisingly enough, they were all okay. A little starved, but they survived. They were certainly happy to have some food and fresh water.

When I left the barn, I looked over to the side of the house where our cellar was buried with snow. The snow was very deep, but I think I could dig down into it to find the cellar door. Grabbing one of Poppa's shovels in the barn, I waded over to the cellar. Of course, I didn't know where Poppa's snowshoes were when I really needed them. With all the strength I could muster, I began digging away mountain upon mountain of snow. I was halfway through, or so I thought, when I heard a voice call out my name.

Lifting my head up, I saw Luke and Uncle Levi hurrying toward me in their snowshoes. They knelt down

beside me from their place on the top of the snow and Uncle
Levi asked, "Are you girls okay?"

I nodded. "Now we are." I told him everything that
had happened.

His face whitened with worry. "Well, how about you
come home with us. We still have some food left."

I shook my head. "No thank you, Uncle Levi. I am
now digging out the cellar and soon we shall have food.
Besides, I should be here for when Poppa and Jesse come
back." Uncle Levi seemed to resign himself to the fact and
Luke stayed to help me dig out the cellar.

Finally, we opened the door. I glanced down into the
darkened cellar, and then proceeded. How wonderful the
sight of canned fruit, dried meat, and canned vegetables
looked! I grabbed a basket that was down there and filled it.
While I was down there, I saw some wood. My scream of
delight brought Luke down, and so he carried up an armful
while I brought the food.

The girls were so thrilled when we walked into the
house. I started a batch of soup, added wood to the fire, and
made a fruit salad to celebrate the ending of a very long
blizzard.

January 25, 1855

Dear Diary,

It seems as though whenever I am outside, someone always comes to meet me. This time, it was Scott. I must admit I was glad to see that he had survived walking home from our barn in the blizzard and he seemed happy to see me still standing!

When he got closer, he asked, "Did you stay out of the barn during the blizzard?"

I smiled. "Well, I went as often as I could, I couldn't let the animals starve!"

At the look on his face, I could tell that he would've liked it if I hadn't gone at all, but still, he didn't argue the fact.

Scott stayed to help me with the barn chores, and while we were inside the barn, I heard the sound of sleigh bells. I froze, not knowing what to think or even say.

Scott was walking to the door, when a voice yelled out, "Carolyn! Bethany! Laura!" It was Jesse!

I uttered a scream of delight and ran out of the barn, well, as fast as I could considering the depth of the snow. Jesse jumped down from the sled and I gave him a big hug. The door from the house opened, and Bethy and Laura appeared. They had quickly dressed in their winter coats and were now dashing through the snow. While Jesse turned to the girls, I climbed in the back of the sleigh next to Poppa.

He gave my braid a tug and smiled at me. "Carrie, I assume you managed through the blizzard all right?"

I laid my hand on his arm, "Oh Poppa, of course. How are you doing?"

Poppa winced as he tried to sit up. "I'll be okay. Jesse can tell you everything."

Bethy and Laura were climbing up next to Poppa then, and I told Jesse why Scott happened to be here. The two talked for a bit, and then I told Jesse everything that had happened.

Both of the boys' eyes widened. "You broke a chair?"

I crossed my arms. "Actually three chairs and don't look so surprised. There was no way we were going to freeze to death in our own house." The shock turned into sheer worry, but I quickly reassured them that everything was okay now.

We got Poppa into the house, and Jesse told me how to care for his wound. It seemed as though Poppa would be laid up in bed for quite a time, and I'm sure he is not at all pleased by that prospect.

January 26, 1855

Dear Diary,

Jesse went out to find some wood he could chop, for he was definitely surprised how we managed for so long on the wood that we had. God was certainly watching over us through everything and he is the one who made our fire wood stretch for as long as it did.

January 27, 1855

Dear Diary,

Jesse and Bethy went into town today to get some supplies, and Uncle Levi and Luke came by to see how we were doing. I could tell they were very relieved that Poppa and Jesse were home, as were we. When Jesse and Bethy got home, they said that the store was pretty much out of everything, but they were trying to ration as much as they could. At least we canned much of our food this year.

January 29, 1855

Dear Diary,

Jesse, Bethy, and Laura went to services this morning, but I stayed home with Poppa. I told him everything that had happened while he and Jesse were gone and how worried I was. He was quiet for a moment, and then told me to get his Bible and open it to Deuteronomy 31:6. It says, *"Be strong and of good courage, do not fear or be afraid; for the Lord your God, He is the One who goes with you. He will not leave you or forsake you."* Poppa told me that God will always be there and he will never leave us, no matter what we are going through.

February 1, 1855

Dear Diary,

It seems hard to believe that it is February after a long month of snow and hardship of January. I am relieved that the month has ended, but I can't help but be worried at what February might bring with it.

February 2, 1855

Dear Diary,

Jesse and some of the other older boys started digging passages through the snow for the school children since school would be starting up tomorrow. When he got back, I had some hot tea waiting for him. Then I asked him how his foot was. Because of the blizzard and Poppa's accident, I had almost forgotten Jesse's hurt foot. He told me that it was much better, for he had rested at the doctor's office while waiting for the blizzard to end. I felt slightly jealous that he got to rest during the blizzard, while I worried about survival, and then I chided myself. Jesse was probably very worried about Poppa and about us at home. I certainly wouldn't have wanted to be in his shoes.

February 3, 1855

Dear Diary,

Jesse, Bethy, and Laura went to school today and it seemed strange to see them go after almost two weeks of having them home with me. Poppa is still in bed, but the doctor visited earlier today and said that he was improving rapidly. I suppose it won't be too long now before he will start working again.

February 6, 1855

Dear Diary,

Since it is Saturday, Bethy helped me in the kitchen today. She made a strawberry rhubarb pie and I made a couple loaves of bread. It felt good to be making food for my

family again and I am still so grateful that God brought us
through that dreadful time.

February 7, 1855

Dear Diary,

We all went to church today, even Poppa, who is just
starting to walk around. Reverend Mast preached on how we
should always give all our concerns to the Lord and he will
take them for us. 1 Peter 5:7 says, *"Casting all your cares upon
Him, for he cares for you."* God cares for us, and as I think back
on this past year of my life, I realize that he really has cared
for me and walked alongside of me every step of the way.

February 9, 1855

Dear Diary,

Poppa is out working in the fields, so now I am by
myself. It seems as though I don't even have sewing to do, for
I finished the blanket I was working on and all the mending
while the girls and I were stuck inside. So instead, I decided
to start writing another book. This one is called Loving
Memories and it will be compiled of stories and memories I
have of Momma.

February 13, 1855

Dear Diary,

I have not written lately in here, because I have been focusing on my latest book. Every time I write something about Momma, I begin crying.

The girls and I did the wash today, which is something we haven't done for a very long time! After the clothes were washed, we did a quick cleaning of the house. Everything is slowly starting to go back to normal.

February 14, 1855

Dear Diary,

Happy *Alla Hjartans dag!* (St. Valentine's Day) It seemed appropriate that the day when we are to show our love to one another, we have church. Reverend Mast preached on John 3:16, which says, *"For God so love the world, that he gave his only Son, that whoever believes in him should not perish but have eternal life"*

February 15, 1855

Dear Diary,

Last night, Bethy, Laura, and I made jelly pastries in

the shape of hearts to take to school. Since *Alla Hjartans dag* fell on a Sunday, they are having the celebration a day later. While they were gone, I took to the kitchen and made bread, cookies, and started a beef roast for supper.

Once the girls were home, they went upstairs to work on their schoolwork and I heard a knock on the door. My surprise was great upon opening it, for it was Sherry Brown. She looked very displeased and said, "Believe me, I would rather not be here, but I have been asked to give this to you." She thrust the small brown package over to me and left quite quickly. I stood in shock, watching her retreat, and then I shut the door and opened my package. What I found was something of great shock to me and I dropped it like it was burning. It was a gold, heart shaped necklace that said *Sweet*. Attached to it was a note that said, *Dear Carolyn, please accept this token of my affections. Cole.* A shivering sensation ran through me. How could he possibly do such a thing? I was only thirteen and after all the mean tricks he played on my sisters and me, he really thinks I would accept such a gift? I walked over to the fire and threw the gift and card in and watched them burn. This action made me feel a little better, but still, my *Alla Hjartans Dag* was ruined.

February 16, 1855

Dear Diary,

I heard a knock on my door again this afternoon. Wondering who it could possibly be this time, I opened it, and found Cole Brown standing there. My first reaction was to slam the door shut, but since I figured that wasn't polite, I left it open. He seemed to have a random smile on his face when he asked me, "What did you think of the necklace? I'm sure you were quite pleased."

Since he had no clue about my feelings, I decided to state them rather bluntly. "Actually, I was very displeased. I thought it an inappropriate gift, one that I shall never wear. As for your affections, I have no need for them, so please, remove them." I said, "Good day", and closed the door. My heart was pounding a mile a minute as I leaned against the closed door. Even though that was rude, what other choice did I have? Taking a deep breath, I went to the kitchen to make supper.

February 17, 1855

Dear Diary,

Poppa's birthday is on March 2, so Jesse and I were

talking last night about what we could possibly give him. After many ideas, we decided to put our money together and send Poppa to Missouri to visit his brother, Philip, who he hasn't seen for seven years. Uncle Philip owns a horse ranch and keeps asking Poppa to visit, but Poppa says he has never had the time to go. I am so excited, for surely we shall surprise Poppa. I only hope we have enough money.

February 18, 1855

Dear Diary,

Unfortunately, I have bad news, but also good news! The bad news is that Jesse was adding things up, and apparently, between the two of us, we don't have enough for the trip. But, the good news is that Jesse rode out to Uncle Levi's place after school to see if they'd like to contribute. They did, so it looks like Poppa's going to Missouri in March!

February 20, 1855

Dear Diary,

Poppa allowed Jesse and I to go into town for some of the groceries that I said I needed. Actually, I mostly wanted to send a telegram to Uncle Phillip to see if our plan would be agreeable to him. Of course, I did bring back a few groceries so I didn't actually tell Poppa a lie, but I can see that it will be hard to keep a secret from him.

February 21, 1855

Dear Diary,

Reverend Mast spoke today on how God is living inside of us, even though he is so big that he created the world. 1 John 4:1-4 says, "*You are of God, little children, and have overcome them, because He who is in you is greater than he who is of the world.*" This verse gives a picture of how great God really is. He lives in me, but he also created me.

February 22, 1855

Dear Diary,

I went on horseback to town today, telling Poppa that I was just going on a ride, but really, I wanted to see if a telegraph had come for me. It was indeed a lovely day for a ride, and it was even better when I found a reply waiting for me at the post office. Uncle Philip had said that he was delighted that Poppa could come and said that he would be eagerly waiting the day of his arrival. I was so excited!

Everything was going according to plan and I just couldn't wait to see Poppa's face when we told him!

February 23, 1855

Dear Diary,

Since I have never included a genealogy in my diary, I suppose it is about time I do so. That way, if my grandchildren read my diary, they will know who all these people are that I am talking about.

George Woodsmall, my poppa, was born in Sweden to Adam and Kathy Woodsmall. He was the second child of four – two brothers and one sister. Philip was the oldest and he and Poppa were always very close growing up. Then, it was Amos and then Kathy.

Amos was the first to marry at a young age and he married Melissa Hintz. Then it was Poppa and Momma. Next, Amos and Melissa had their first son, George. Then Jesse was born to Momma and Poppa. Then Mildred was born, and not long after her birth, Philip left for America. There was much sadness when he left, even though I wasn't even born to know about it.

Not long after that, I was born, and I believe that if I

was a boy, my name would've been Philip. Bethany came next and then Amos, and then Aunt Kathy married Cain Hardy. Poppa, Momma, Amos, and Melissa didn't approve of her match at all. Cain Hardy came from a rougher sort of family and they thought that he would mistreat her. But thankfully, nothing has happened so far. Laura was born, and then Charity, Kathy and Cain's first child. Unfortunately, it looked as though Charity was born before it was time, but Kathy argues that she just came early. Momma and Melissa know the truth, but Charity's birth isn't much talked about in our family.

Then, the time came for us to move to America. After much agonizing, Poppa and Momma decided that it would be better to move their family to America. They tried to convince Amos and Melissa to come with them, but they firmly said that they didn't want to go. At first, we were planning on settling near Uncle Philip's place, but somehow it was decided that it would be better to do so near the Holbrooks, but I have already wrote about that story.

February 24, 1855

Dear Diary,

Now, I shall write all about Momma's family. Juliana Cradle, my momma, was also born in Sweden, to Kale and Charity Cradle. She was the middle child, in between two brothers, Kaleb and Levi.

Kaleb was the first to marry, and he married Marylou Shetz. Next, Levi married Maria Schmidt, and finally, Momma married Poppa.

My cousin Kale was the first of the cousins to be born, and he was born to Kaleb and Marylou. Next was Herb, Levi and Maria's first son, and then Mort, Kaleb and Marylou's second son. Then came Jesse, then Luke, me, Kirsten, Bethany, and Laura. Not long after Laura's birth, Poppa and Momma, along with Levi and Maria, decided to move to America. Mr. Holbrook, Poppa, and Uncle Levi were good friends growing up, which is why we eventually settled with the Holbrooks. Poppa and Levi also decided that Minnesota was a little more cultured than Missouri probably was.

Well, that is my family. Not too big, but just the right size. I often wonder if any more of my family will come to America. I would truly love it if Mille came, but I would love it too if anyone would come. Momma always told me that they were all stuck in their ways and didn't want to change.

February 26, 1855

Dear Diary,

I rode horseback into town today, for I didn't really need any big items, just wanted to check the mail. To my genuine happiness, I received a letter from Millie. I could hardly wait till I got home to read it, but I did. It read:

Dearest Carolyn,

Oh my! I haven't written you for so long, and here, you have sent me multiple letters! When you wrote those letters about the blizzard, I sat in my house by the fire, shivering. I must say, I made quite the sight. George was coming in from outside and when he saw me, he thought I was sick. I assured him that I was quite well, but he was quite cold after I told him what happened to you too!

I do hope that everyone is back to normal at your place and that your Poppa and Jesse aren't still laid up, though by the lateness of this letter, I'm sure everyone is fine as ever...

Her letter went on for quite some time, giving detail to every little thing that happened in Sweden over the course of these past months. How I long to be able to see Millie again!

Season 4

March 1, 1855

Dear Diary,

Tomorrow is Poppa's birthday, and the day after that, he will be leaving for Missouri. We told Poppa about the gift yesterday so that he could start packing and make any necessary plans. He was so surprised and he said he couldn't go and leave us, but we managed to convince him. He looked so excited at the prospect of seeing Uncle Philip!

March 2, 1855

Dear Diary,

Since it is Poppa's birthday today and he is leaving tomorrow, I spent the day in the kitchen making the most wonderful supper possible! I made a beef roast with potatoes and carrots, red beets, green beans, applesauce, and bread. For dessert we had carrot cake, raspberry pudding, and double chocolate chip cookies. Uncle Levi, Aunt Maria, Luke, and Kirsten came over for supper, and we all had a wonderful time, although birthdays are always hard to celebrate with Momma not here.

March 3, 1855

Dear Diary,

We all loaded up in the wagon early this morning and took Poppa into town. I didn't think I would cry when he boarded the train, but I did shed some tears. I can't believe it will be two long weeks till we see Poppa again. It almost seems like we will never see him again, but I know that is not true. I told myself that this trip was pretty much my idea! We will be fine and Poppa will get to see his brother again.

March 7, 1855

Dear Diary,

Reverend Mast talked today about how God is always there when we need him. He will answer our calls and he will keep us safe. Psalm 4:8 says, "*In peace I will both lie down and sleep; for you alone, O Lord, make me dwell in safety.*" This verse just gives me such a comforting feeling knowing that God is watching over me when I am awake and when I am sleeping. He is watching over Poppa and *Mormor* and Millie and all my family from all over the world. Such a wonderful feeling!

March 8, 1855

Dear Diary,

When I woke up this morning, I had this strange feeling come over me, and I thought perhaps that I was getting sick. Of course, I would never tell anything of the like to Jesse, because he would just worry unnecessarily about me. So after they left for school, I made myself a cup of peppermint tea and tried to rest my aching head. To no avail, my eyes just wanted to close and I did allow myself to take a short nap, but I had to get supper going for Jesse and the girls would be home before long.

March 11, 1855

Dear Diary,

As you may have suspected, I have been in bed for the past two days with a very bad fever and a cut on my head. On the ninth, I still wasn't feeling good, but I went outside to close the barn door since Jesse had left it open. Walking out there made me so exhausted that I just had to go and rest a bit. I could feel my head starting to spin but I knew I had to get to the house before I fainted. Unfortunately, when I stood up, I came crashing to the ground with a thud. Groaning, I lifted my hand to my head and felt the warm sensation of blood and then I knew that this was serious. I pressed my shawl against my head, trying to stop the bleeding, but it didn't work. Desperate, I called for Lucia, who came when I called her because I had forgotten to latch her stall door! I draped my bloody shawl over her neck, and told her to go to the school. She has gone there so many times, that she now knows the way and the word!

I don't know how long I was lying there, but it seemed like forever. Suddenly, I heard footsteps in the doorway of the barn and I knew Jesse had come to me. I moaned to let him know where I was, and Jesse and Luke ran over to me. They both knelt by me, and Jesse gingerly touched my head. In an urgent voice he told Luke to hitch up the wagon, and he said to me, "Don't worry, Carrie, you'll be all right." His voice was strained and I could tell that he was desperately worried. I tried to smile and reassure him, but my mouth didn't want to obey my head. Then, Jesse carefully picked me up and laid me in the back of the wagon and I blacked out.

I don't remember anything else that happened after that, but Bethy told me that Jesse and Luke drove me to the doctor's office and that I had a very bad fever. Doctor Richards said that I could go home, but someone had to be looking after me at all times. So that is where I am today. Aunt Maria comes over during the day, and Bethy, Laura, and Kirsten take turns in the evening. I haven't gotten through many days yet, but at least they sorted everything out!

March 12, 1855

Dear Diary,

After school let out, Jesse rode into town to see if there was any news from Poppa. There was none, but there was a letter from our cousin George Woodsmall. Surprisingly enough, he didn't even open it, but waited for me to do the honors. So while I lay in bed, Jesse, Bethy, and Laura crowded around me to see what George had to say. It read:

Dear Uncle George, Jesse, Carolyn, Bethany, and Laura,

I hope this letter finds you all in good health. I'm afraid that I'm not much of a writer, so this letter won't be quite as long as my sister's letters are. I'm sure Millie has told you all about Phoebe Star, and I am happy to say that we have just gotten engaged. After discussing the possibilities, we have decided that we would like to settle in America, preferably Minnesota. I am writing this letter wondering if you would be able to check around and see if there is any land for sale that I would be able to buy.

I almost forgot, Poppa and Momma send their greetings and tell you that they will write soon. I look forward to hearing from you,

George Woodsmall

I could hardly believe what I was reading. After hearing so much about George and Phoebe from Millie, I found myself wondering when they would indeed get married. Now, they are and they want to move here! I can't help but wonder if Millie and the rest of the family would come along. Now that would be wonderful!!

March 13, 1855

Dear Diary,

Since it is a Saturday, I was pretty much by myself today because Aunt Maria stayed at her house and Bethy and Laura were doing all the housework. From my place in the loft, I couldn't quite hear everything going on, but I yelled down quite often making sure they were doing everything the way they were supposed to.

Around lunchtime, I peered out the window and saw Scott Harp talking to my brother. Scott handed something to Jesse, rousing my curiosity. I wanted to bang on the window, but I was afraid that would embarrass me too much. Instead, I tried to wait as patiently as I could inside until Jesse finally walked inside. I called him up immediately, and from the expectant look on my face, he knew I was spying on him. Without saying much, he handed me a closed letter. I looked up at him. "Why didn't you open it?"

He shrugged, sitting on the edge of my bed. "You're a much better letter reader." It was a telegram and I opened up and quickly read:

My dear children, I am afraid that Uncle Philip has been in a dreadful accident and I must stay to help him for a while. I'm not sure how long I will be gone, but it will be longer than two weeks.

Thank you for word on Carolyn. Make sure she stays off her feet as long as possible. All my love, Poppa.

How dreadful for Poppa! I wish I had convinced Jesse not to tell Poppa about my illness, but then again, I think I was unconscious when he made the decision. I'm sure Uncle Philip needs Poppa much more than I do right now. I have my wonderful siblings looking out for me and Poppa needn't worry, for Jesse isn't letting me move a muscle!

March 14, 1855

Dear Diary,

Jesse and Bethy went to services today and Laura stayed home to be with me. I tried to tell Jesse that I would be fine on my own, but he didn't listen. Nevertheless, I did enjoy the time that I was able to spend with Laura. I told her to get my Bible and we read together out of 2 Corinthians. Chapter 9 verse 6 says, *"But this I say: He who sows sparingly will also reap sparingly, and he who sows bountifully, will also reap bountifully."* By reading this verse, God is telling us that we should spend much time studying his word, for the more we know, the more we can grow and produce and harvest good works. When I tried explaining it to Laura, I could tell she still didn't understand, and I'm not sure I quite do either, but I just have to rely that God will show me when the time is right.

March 15, 1855

Dear Diary,

My fever is finally gone and the cut on my head is healing quite nicely. Jesse inspected me in the evening and told me that he would take me to the doctor tomorrow. I was so excited! I am longing to get out of bed and cook and clean, though I never thought I would actually say those words aloud.

March 16, 1855

Dear Diary,

My appointment went very well today, and Doctor Richards said I could start doing some more work, but not quite as much as I used to. I grudgingly agreed, at least it was better than nothing.

March 18, 1855

Dear Diary,

I decided to go on a ride today since it has been so long since I have been out. Surely a calm horseback ride isn't too strenuous; still I didn't ask Jesse's permission, for he surely would've said no. I rode all around and surprisingly enough, I ended up near the Bows' house. Mrs. Bow saw me outside and invited me in for a cup of tea, which I was all too glad to accept. We talked a little, and she asked how I was feeling, for she said that she had heard in church this past Sunday that I had hit my head pretty hard. I told her that I was feeling much better and that this was my first ride in a very long time.

All too soon, it was time for me to go, but before I did, she invited us for supper on Saturday evening. "I've wanted to invite you all over ever since your Poppa went to Missouri, but you can plainly see how the time has gotten away from me!" I laughed and said that we would love to come for supper.

March 19, 1855

Dear Diary,

I did a little bit of everything today, or so it seemed. This morning, I was in the kitchen making bread and figuring out what to make for supper. Then I took a break and did some sewing, for I needed to hem one of Bethy's dresses so that it would fit Laura. The girls are about the same size now which is sometimes hard to believe how fast they are growing! After I made lunch for myself, I did some cleaning. Just a bit, mind you, and it didn't tire me one bit. Now I am finally sitting down, and it gives me a lovely, comfortable feeling to have accomplished something worthwhile. Ever so much better than lounging in bed thinking about every little possible thing that comes into my head!

March 20, 1855

Dear Diary,

Jesse rode into town today and the girls and I did some sewing. When he got back, there was a telegram from Poppa. Jesse gave it to me, and I read:

My dear children, I will be home on April 3. Uncle Philip is doing much better, and I am anxious to be home with you all. Stay out of trouble and if you need anything go to Uncle Levi's. All my love, Poppa.

We all cheered. How happy we were that Poppa would be coming home soon. I am so excited and very relieved that Uncle Philip is doing much better. I know Poppa felt pulled in two directions, and I'm sure that staying with Uncle Philip was the right decision.

That evening, we had supper with the Bow family. It was a very delicious dinner, and I enjoyed talking with Heather and Mrs. Bow. It felt different to be eating someplace without Momma and Poppa. We were just getting used to going places without Momma, and now Poppa is gone too, though I keep telling myself that it is only for a little while longer. Soon, Poppa will be home.

March 21, 1855

Dear Diary,

Reverend Mast spoke today on how God will never abandon us; he will always be with us. Psalm 16:1-2, *"Preserve me, O God, for in you I take refuge. I say to the Lord, 'You are my Lord; I have no good apart from you.'"* When we are apart from God, nothing good will happen to us. But even if we don't talk to him and try to push him away, He is always right there just waiting for us to call him back.

March 22, 1855

Dear Diary,

Today has been such an awful day! First, I couldn't figure out what to make, but finally I got some soup together.

Then when I needed to add more logs to the stove, our pile was empty. I searched and searched, but to no avail, there were no logs cut. So there I went, out to the woods to do a man's job of cutting wood. I was tired, sweaty, and hungry when I finally finished lugging back all the pieces to the house. On top of all that, when I went in the house my fire was out and the soup was cold. It wouldn't take too long to heat up, but I knew supper was going to be later that normal.

I had just gone out to bring more logs inside, when Jesse came home by himself and told me that the girls went home with Caddie and Julie and that we were all invited to the Harp's for supper. I crossed my arms at him. "And I suppose you said yes."

He shrugged. "Of course, I never turn down a meal."

I threw the pile of logs that I was holding down on the ground. "And what do you think I've been doing all day long? Do you know the struggle it has been to prepare supper tonight? Now no one will even eat it!" I was furious and I could tell that Jesse was taken aback by my mood.

"I'm dreadfully sorry, but I thought you enjoy going to someone else's house to eat." His voice dripped with sarcasm and his face showed that he was starting to get mad at me.

I should just tell him that I would go and just save

supper for later, but I turned on my heel and marched toward the house.

He yelled after me, "Where are you going?"

I yelled right back, "Inside to eat the supper I made!"

"Fine, the girls and I will eat over at the Harp's."

I slammed the door shut after his last words. As soon as I did, I wanted to reopen it and tell him I was sorry and that I would go. But I didn't. I was too stubborn and I didn't want to give in first.

It was late before they got back. I was on the couch trying to read, but I couldn't seem to concentrate. Bethy and Laura must have noticed that something was amiss between Jesse and me because they were very quiet. Laura asked why I was sitting without any fire.

Very curtly, I replied, "That would be because there is no wood and I only chopped enough to keep my soup hot." I do believe that was the last conversation of the night. Jesse stormed upstairs to his side of the loft and the girls followed suit.

Sitting down here alone, I have much to think back on. I should've done things differently, and I don't know why I didn't.

March 23, 1855

Dear Diary,

I woke up to the house cold and Jesse was already gone. Getting dressed, I didn't know where he could've possibly gone, but I was going out to chop some more wood. My bad day from yesterday was just carrying over. Since it was still early, it was quite chilly. I hurried to the woods, but as I got to the edge, I saw Jesse chopping wood. Suddenly, all the pride I had vanished and I felt dreadful for the way I had treated him. Surely he must've been busy and didn't have any time to cut us some more wood, but that was no way to treat him. Momma would've been appalled. As I was standing there, a verse came to my mind, one that Momma often quoted. It is Ephesians 4:26, *"Be angry and do not sin; do not let the sun go down on your anger."*

I knew what I had to do then, so slowly I walked over to Jesse. When I gently laid my hand on his arm, I felt him jump. He looked over at me.

I took a deep breath, "Listen, Jesse, I'm really sorry for how I treated you yesterday. It was just a bad day and I shouldn't have taken that anger out on you. I'm sorry."

His eyes studied mine, "I only thought that you would

be relieved to not have to make supper, but..."

I jumped in, "I know that now, and I usually am. But that was just a bad day and I will never do it again!"

Jesse's face broke into a smile. "You didn't let me finish. I was going to say that I can see what you mean, and I shouldn't have sprung it on you that very day."

I couldn't help but smile as well and I gave him a hug. "Let's never fight again, especially about something so silly."

He agreed, and then regarded me with a funny expression, "Did you really come out here and swing this big ax over your head?"

I rolled my eyes at him. "Of course I did. I did it before, and I didn't want to starve. Since you obviously don't believe me, I'll show you." I grabbed the ax from him and proceeded to chop the wood into pieces that would fit into the stove.

Looking back, it all ended well, but I wish I would've remembered Momma's advice sooner, for it would've spared all of us much grief. At least it was a growing experience, for now I shall endeavor never to lose my temper again.

March 24, 1855

Dear Diary,

Jesse rode into town this afternoon, and when he came back, he brought a letter from Millie. I was so excited to hear from my dear cousin, that I dropped all that I was doing and went up to the loft to read it. It said:

Dearest Carolyn,

I suppose you have heard the wonderful news that my brother is finally engaged! I can hardly believe it myself even though I have tried for so long. Momma is just about bursting with happiness and Phoebe seems to glow whenever she comes over. I can tell Farmor is excited too, even though she doesn't show it as much as Momma does. Phoebe has asked me to be her bridesmaid and I am about bouncing off the wall! I am so excited that I am going to have such a wonderful sister!

Oh! I almost forgot the even better news! Well, I suppose it is sad and good news at the same time. I'm assuming George has told you all that he and Phoebe are moving to America. I am excited at this, because maybe, just maybe, Momma and Poppa will agree to go too and then I shall see you again! But if they do not agree, it means that I shall not see Phoebe again either. I even went as far as seeing if they would let just me go with George and Phoebe, but then I shall not see Momma and Poppa again. Oh, I do not know

203

what I want! Momma hasn't given an answer either way, so I have some time to figure out what I truly want.

I hope all is going well for you and your family. Farmor relayed to us that your Poppa is visiting Uncle Philip. When she told us, she got this sad tone in her voice and I could tell then that she truly does miss you all. Sometimes it is hard to tell with Farmor because she never expresses her feelings, but that day was different.

Do write soon and tell me everything that is happening. I cannot believe that I have just filled up a letter to you all about my brother!! Oh well, I'm sure you can tell how excited I am.

Until we meet again (which hopefully will be very soon), I remain your cousin

Millie

I can't believe it. Millie actually asked her parents if she could come here with George and Phoebe! I ran down and told the girls and Jesse the news. They all just laughed at my excitement, but really, this is so very, very exciting!!

March 25, 1855

Dear Diary,

Aunt Maria stopped by this afternoon with a telegram. I took it from her quickly, wondering what it could possibly contain. It said:

My dear children, Uncle Philip has just died. I'm hoping to still come home on the third, but I am not certain yet. Stay strong, my dear ones, everything will turn out all right. All my love, Poppa.

I couldn't keep back the tears that were starting to gather in my eyes. Why, oh why, would I cry when I don't even know who Uncle Philip really is? Well, I guess I know him, I just don't know what he was like. We've received letters from him now and again, but nothing too descriptive. Aunt Maria climbed down from the wagon and wrapped me in her arms, "Shh, Carolyn, it will be okay." I knew it would be, for me at least, but from Poppa's note, I could just tell that he was hurting so much.

First, Momma and Herb died within weeks of each other, and during that same time, Grandpa Woodsmall died in Sweden. Momma's death was so painful; it was hard for all of us to bear that. Grandpa's death was difficult for Poppa as well, because I know he wished he could've been there. Now Poppa's brother, whom he was the closest with, died too. I'm sure he wishes that he went earlier to visit and that he sent more letters, but the past can't be undone. I'm only glad that Poppa was there for Uncle Philip. Sometimes, I can't help but ask God, why? Why are all these horrible things happening to our family? I suppose death will never end, but might it just take a break so that we can catch our breath?

March 26, 1855

Dear Diary,

Today was the last day of school and Bethy, Laura, and Jesse all came home quite glad that it was over if just for a season. Laura was glad to play outside again, Bethy to be indoors sewing, and I'm sure Jesse is happy just to be out of the schoolhouse. I can hardly believe that he shall never go to school again. It makes him seem quite old, though I suppose that I am getting old too since he is only two years older than me. I am glad that school has ended and I will have the girls to help me with all the housework, even though I have gotten used to it all by now!

March 27, 1855

Dear Diary,

Jesse went out to the fields today to begin the spring planting. He was going to wait for Poppa to start plowing, but with the untimely delays, we both decided to get started. After lunch, Laura and I went out to help Jesse, and Bethy stayed behind at the house to start supper. By the end of the day, the entire field was plowed and part of it was seeded.

March 29, 1855

Dear Diary,

It was a nice day today, not too cold and not too hot. Laura and I were working out in the garden. We got all the dead stalks and plants pulled out and were starting working on tilling it up so that it would be ready to plant. All of a sudden, I heard a wagon pull up and we both looked up. Poppa was there, with Mr. Harp and Scott. "Poppa!" We both jumped up and ran over to the wagon where Poppa was.

He jumped down and engulfed us both in a hug. "Oh my sweet girls! A month is far too long to be separated!"

I pulled back and looked up at him. "How did you get here?"

He laughed. "I got an early ride here, and the Harps just happened to see me walking through town with my luggage." Bethy came running out of the house and I could see Jesse coming in from the fields as well. This was one of the happiest days ever. Poppa was home and we were together again.

March 30, 1855

Dear Diary,

Laura and I began planting our garden and Poppa and
Jesse went out to the fields. It felt so good to have Poppa
home again. Aunt Maria invited us over for dinner tonight,
and during dinner, Poppa retold all the adventures he had
while in Missouri. He told us that Uncle Philip was actually
injured by one of his horses who threw him off and trampled
him. The weight of that horse came down on top of him and
crushed one of his lungs. The doctor thought that it might be
possible he could survive, but nevertheless, he didn't. While
he was unable to move, Poppa oversaw Uncle Philip's horse
ranch making sure that everything was running in tip top
order. Then, after his death, he sold the ranch for a handsome
sum of money and sent that money to *Farmor* in Sweden. I
wish that Poppa had brought some of the horses back with
him, but I can see how it would be better for them to stay as a
whole for the next buyer.

April 1, 1855

Dear Diary,

The girls and I did the wash today, and I must say, it

has been quite some time now since I have done it. Bethy told me that she and Laura had done the wash while I was quite unable to do it and I am so proud of them. I can hardly believe that my little sisters did the wash without me to guide them! I was almost ready to shirk my responsibilities today, but I enjoy spending time with them.

April 2, 1855

Dear Diary,

The girls went to Caddie and Julie's house to play for the day, and with Poppa and Jesse out in the fields, I decided to take advantage of the quiet house and write some more in my book. As I sat and thought about what to write next about my memories of Momma, something came to me. It happened about six months before her death. One Sunday afternoon I was helping Momma clean up the dishes. I told her, "Momma, I need to tell you something. I don't want to be the normal housewife who does only cleaning and cooking for her family. I want to be a famous author and travel the world. Is that wrong?"

Momma continued washing the dishes. "No, Carolyn, it is not wrong. Keeping a family is a notable and praiseworthy job, but you don't need to feel like that is your only option. You're young yet, but I think as time goes by, you'll see that you can do both things at once."

As the memory came back to me, tears clouded my vision. Here I was, keeping house and writing. I wasn't traveling the world, but that might come. Taking care of my family is an important job as Momma had said, and it is possible to do both.

April 4, 1855

Dear Diary,

Today is Palm Sunday. Reverend Mast preached on Jesus' coming into Jerusalem. Everyone praised him and laid palm branches and their coats down for him to walk on. The people thought that he was the king coming to save them and overthrow the Romans. In time, he would, but he had a greater purpose to accomplish--saving the people from their sins. *"Hosanna to the Son of David. Blessed is he who comes in the name of the Lord. Hosanna to the highest!"* Matthew 21:9.

April 6, 1855

Dear Diary,

When Poppa came home today from the fields, he told me that he saw Mr. Brown and invited their family over for Easter dinner. I was appalled, but I tried not to let it show. Of all the people, Poppa would have to invite the Browns over here for dinner. The bullies were coming to my house. The word slipped into my mind before I could stop it. I must try to be nice, but I'm sure Sherry and Cole will criticize my entire meal.

April 7, 1855

Dear Diary,

Well, Poppa must really enjoy inviting people, for when he went into town today, he saw Mrs. Miller and invited her and her boys to our dinner. I am much more pleased with this arrangement than the last, but I can't help but have this feeling that Poppa has taken a liking to Mrs. Miller. I try not to think about it much, but sometimes I just can't help it!

April 8, 1855

Dear Diary,

The girls and I worked out a menu of everything we have to make and the things that other people are bringing. Here is what we have planned out so far:

~ Ham - me

~ Scalloped potatoes - me

~ Green Beans - me

~ Carrots – Aunt Maria

~ Corn – Aunt Maria

~ Bread - me

~ Red Beets - Mrs. Brown

~ Strawberry Pie - Aunt Maria

~ Cherry Pie - Widow Miller

~ Pumpkin Pie – me

Aunt Maria told me that if we needed any help, she and Kirsten could come by on Saturday to help us, but I told her that we would be fine. I've made dinners before, and this isn't even as much.

April 9, 1855

Dear Diary,

Today is *Langfredag* (Good Friday). We don't have a service to attend, so Poppa read to us from Matthew 27:11-61, which was Jesus' crucifixion. For a long time, I've wondered why this day was always referred to as "Good" Friday. What good is it when someone is being killed? But now I realize the answer. That 'someone' is God's son and he died so that we might be saved. Now that is something very good indeed that has happened.

April 10, 1855

Dear Diary,

Since today is the day before Easter, the girls and I have been busy from sunup to sundown cooking and cleaning to get our house ready for company. After taking the rugs out for a good beating, mopping, and dusting, the house looked super clean! Then, we started making ham, bread, and the pumpkin pie. Poppa and Jesse went outside and set up two long tables for all our guests to sit at. We have lots of people coming--Uncle Levi, Aunt Maria, Luke, Kirsten, Mrs. Miller, Henry, Jake, Mr. Brown, Mrs. Brown, Brent, Cole,

Sherry, and the five of us.

April 11, 1855

Dear Diary,

Early this morning, I awoke and started making my scalloped potatoes, green beans, and reheating the ham. Then, we all went to the church service and Reverend Mast preached on Jesus' resurrection from the dead. Sometimes, I wonder how it would have been to be one of the Marys and find that Jesus was not in the tomb, but he was alive! It would be mind-boggling, especially since they just witnessed his death on Friday. Matthew 28:5-6, *"But the angel said to the women, 'Do not be afraid, for I know that you seek Jesus who was crucified. He is not here, for he has risen, as he said.'"*

After the service, we went home and finished getting everything ready for the meal. This is one day I wish Momma were here, for she always knew how to keep calm even when everything was going crazy! Aunt Maria and Uncle Levi arrived first, then the Millers, and finally the Browns. Thankfully, I never had to sit next to Cole, but I could feel his eyes watching me.

When I brought my pumpkin pie out, Sherry said

quite loudly, "What is that? It looks burnt."

A thick silence fell upon everyone. I met Sherry's gaze and answered quite calmly, "It is a pumpkin pie--my mother's recipe." Then I proceeded to set the pie down and cut slices for everyone.

While I was cutting, Kirsten slid next to me and whispered, "How did you manage to stay so composed? I'm afraid I would've thrown the pie in her face."

I whispered back, "The thought crossed my mind."

We smiled, and proceeded to serve.

When the dinner was finished, Bethy, Laura, Kirsten, and I proceeded to the kitchen to wash all the dishes.

As soon as I turned the water on to start washing, Laura said, "May I please go throw these extra potatoes in Sherry's face? She deserves it."

I handed Laura a dish to dry. "There is no sense in repaying hatred with anger. For some reason, Sherry dislikes me very much, and I don't quite like her myself, but there is no need to play a cruel trick."

Bethy took the dry dish from Laura and put it away. "That sounds like something Momma would've said." I exchanged a smile with Bethy, for I had thought that myself. If Momma wants me to teach the girls, I had better not be teaching them to revenge others just because they hurt their feelings.

Kirsten chimed in, "I still think we should think of something to do. She's going to keep doing this until she hurts you big time."

I sighed, "There is nothing to do. Forget about it and perhaps she will as well." I could tell Kirsten and Laura still wanted to do something more, but at least for the time being, nothing was said.

April 12, 1855

Dear Diary,

It might seem strange that we cleaned after a dinner, but that is exactly what we did. The house was a mess after people walking through it, and even though we ate outside, my kitchen was a disaster. We weren't able to clean up the entire kitchen last night, so I told the girls we would finish up today, which was exactly what we did.

April 13, 1855

Dear Diary,

The girls went on a walk today, so it was my job to

take water to Poppa and Jesse in the fields. When I got back to the house, I saw Cole Brown riding toward me. I was uncertain what I should do, so I held the bucket tightly against me and waited to see what he had to say. He stayed atop his horse, which irks me to no end. Why does he think he is so much better than me that he has to be above me?

He nodded his head as a greeting. "Sherry's comment about your pie was uncalled for. I think the entire meal was very good." His niceness caught me off guard.

"Thank you." I waited to see what else he wanted.

What he said next shocked me. "You know, I think we would get along well together. Here." He handed me a necklace and when I took it, I saw that it had the word "love" written on it.

I shoved it back at him, "I will not accept this. I am only thirteen and I have no interest in you at all."

When he wouldn't take back his necklace, I threw it to the ground and walked away. I heard him call after me, "You will regret this decision, Carolyn Woodsmall. Mark my words you will! Not every man wants a girl who hasn't completed her schooling and is devoted to taking care of her younger siblings."

His threatening words hit me to the core and I became

afraid at what he might do next. When I heard his horse whinny, I dropped my bucket and ran into the house. His words kept ringing in my head over and over again. I dropped to the floor in front of the door, shaking with tears streaming down my face. I didn't know what to do. Was his threat real? Something in the back of my head told me that he really would do something, because that is the kind of person that he is.

I heard footsteps on the porch and then the door knob turned. I leapt to my feet yelling, "Don't come in!" I threw myself against the door, fearing that it was Cole trying to come inside.

To my relief, it was Jesse. "Carolyn? Is that you? It's me."

"Jesse!" I screamed and fell away from the door. I must've looked a fright, for when Jesse walked in his face turned white with worry.

He came over to me and grasped my shoulders, "What's wrong? Poppa wanted me to tell you that he was heading to town for something, but I can get him."

I tried to control all my emotions and quickly told Jesse what happened. His face grew dark and he turned and strode out the door. I ran after him and grabbed his arm,

"Where are you going?"

"To tell Cole Brown not to come near you and if I ever see his face again, I'll punch it!"

I gasped. "Don't you think that will make matters worse? Why don't you wait for Poppa?"

He didn't answer me, and rode off toward the Brown place.

Jesse came back before Poppa, still in one piece. He told me that I didn't have to worry about anything, but I still wasn't quite sure. I told Poppa when he got home and he said he was going to talk to Mr. Brown, but I pleaded with him not to. "There is no reason to cause more trouble." I guess Poppa agreed with me, for he didn't talk to Mr. Brown that I am aware of.

April 14, 1855

Dear Diary,

I am trying my hardest to forget what Cole said to me. I decided that baking might lift my mood, so I made *pepparkokor* this morning. Jesse, Poppa, and the girls were very excited, for it is a favorite dessert in our family.

April 17, 1855

Dear Diary,

I was busy in the garden this afternoon, when Jesse and Scott rode in. I had sent Jesse into town for some grocery items and it didn't surprise me in the least that he returned with a friend. They both hopped down and came over to me.

Jesse held out a letter, "You will never believe who wrote you, Carolyn."

I wiped my hands on my apron and reached for the letter. "Millie? *Mormor? Farmor?*"

Jesse regarded that letter. "No, it is from California. Who lives in California, Carrie?"

My eyes lit up. "I can't believe! I never thought I would hear back from them!"

Jesse and Scott asked at the same time, "Who?"

I grabbed the letter and looked at the address. "Don't you remember? Back in December, I wrote to Mrs. Holbrook. I never thought I would hear back, especially since I didn't have an address. But look!" I quickly opened it. It said:

Dear Carolyn,

How lovely to hear from you. I meant to write you, truly I did, but I guess I just got too busy. Anyhow, I'm truly sorry to hear about the loss of your mother. Actually, my mother died also about a year ago. Father says that it was the trip out to California that eventually weakened her, but she did get sick as well.

Caleb hit a gold pile, and we are now living in a nice big house in San Francisco. Daniel and I go to a fancy school too. You should really convince your family to come out here. It is much nicer living like this compared to farming and having barely enough money to survive.

Feel free to write me again. I would be glad to hear from you and stay in touch.

Your friend,

Marie

I found myself staring at the letter long after it was finished.

Jesse let out a low whistle, "Wow. They're rich and completely changed."

Scott said, "Who wouldn't want to earn a living? It's better than being stuck inside all day."

Jesse turned to me, "Why did you write them, Carrie?"

I put the letter back in the envelope. "I thought that since Momma and Mrs. Holbrook had been such good friends, it would be nice to write her about her death. You know, Marie and I used to be close as well. But I doubt that I shall write her back. I don't need to hear about all her riches."

Jesse and Scott both laughed.

I find it hard to believe that friends that you have held so high up can just fade within seconds. I mean, it was only a year and a half ago since they left, and five years ago we came here to live with them! My, how things do change!

April 18, 1855

Dear Diary,

Reverend Mast spoke about God creating a new heaven and a new earth. Isaiah 65:17 says, *"For behold, I create new heavens and a new earth, and the former things shall not be remembered or come into mind."* How wonderful it is to know that one day there will be a new heaven and a new earth. And nothing shall be known; I take that as meaning there will be no more suffering, no more hatred, and no more pain. It shall be a wonderful day!

April 20, 1855

Dear Diary,

Kirsten came by today while I was in the kitchen making bread. She ran in and exclaimed, "Guess what, Carolyn?"

I turned around. "What?"

She clasped her hand together. "Momma and Poppa said that we could host a spring party! Isn't that thrilling?"

I told her that it was, and we talked all about it. She told me there would be dancing and wonderful food. I was so excited! The date is set for Saturday, May first, at noon.

April 21, 1855

Dear Diary,

I searched through my trunk today and found my ball dress from the Christmas dance. I decided that it would do very nicely if I added a bit of lace to change it up, for I couldn't ask Poppa to buy me a new ball dress again. Plus, I wouldn't have enough time to make one, since the dance is just two weeks away.

April 22, 1855

Dear Diary,

Ever since Poppa returned home from Missouri, he has been looking for land for George and Phoebe to buy. He hasn't had any luck yet, for at the present, no one is interested in selling. I am fairly confident that something will come up.

It has to come up! After all the good things Millie has said about Phoebe, I want to meet her!

April 23, 1855

Dear Diary,

With the weather being so nice, I decided to take a horseback ride into town. Originally, I would've just ridden through the woods, but I wanted to stay in the sun. When I got to town, I discovered that there was a letter for me. This one was from Millie. It read:

Dearest Carolyn,

So Poppa and Momma have said that they will not be moving to America any time soon, which means I have tried a different tactic. I started pleading with them to allow only me to come to America with George and Phoebe.

Do you know how hard it is to convince your parents to send you to America? Probably not, but it is very, very hard. George says I can as long as Momma and Poppa pay for me and Phoebe says yes because she would like some help around the place and sisterly companionship. Poppa says he can't spare the money, and Momma cries and says a flat no.

Speaking of money, you know that large sum of money your father sent to Farmor? Well, she has agreed to split it evenly

amongst all her grandchildren. Can you believe it? It is certainly
something I never expected. Now, Poppa can't complain about the
money. If only he and Momma would come as well! I'm sure they
would be happy there!

Nevertheless, all we can do is keep praying. I am confident I
shall see you someday, though soon isn't looking very likely.

I remain your affectionate cousin,

Millie

I am so excited that Millie is actually considering
coming to America, but I don't know how she could stand to
live away from her parents for so long of a time. I don't think
I could bear living away from Poppa, especially not an ocean
away! Good thing I don't have to.

April 24, 1855

Dear Diary,

The girls are going back to school on Monday, and I'm
getting quite sad just thinking of it. Only girls and little boys
go to school in the spring and summer. At least Jesse will be
home, but I'll still be lonely without Bethy and Laura.

April 26, 1855

Dear Dairy,

The girls are at school and the house seems extra quiet today. Poppa and Jesse are out in the fields and they only come in for lunch, so I am pretty much on my own. I decided to do some writing in my book. After writing all morning, I spent the afternoon in the kitchen making bread, beef stew, and a cherry pie for supper tonight.

When the girls came home, they told me all that was happening in school. First of all, there was a new teacher. Miss Pearson is her name, and Bethy said she is very sweet-tempered and knows a lot. Laura said that she can even control the younger, rambunctious boys. I couldn't help but smile at all their descriptions. Even though I wasn't there, I was glad they had a good time.

April 28, 1855

Dear Diary,

Today I was sewing when Mrs. Miller came by. She said that she was just passing by and decided to visit with me, if I wasn't too busy. I told her that I wasn't and invited her inside. I made some tea and we visited. I truly felt like a lady, and Mrs. Miller treated me like one. She is not that bad, now that I am spending more time with her. I just don't think I would want her as my mother.

April 29, 1855

Dear Diary,

I made chocolate oatmeal raisin cookies today. They are a favorite in our house; though, it seems as if every cookie I make is a favorite! Luke came by, and I asked him if there was anything I could do to help get ready for the dance. He shook his head, grabbed a cookie, and went outside to find Jesse. Yes, those cookies are even a favorite of Luke's.

April 30, 1855

Dear Diary,

I can hardly believe that the dance is really tomorrow! It came upon me so quickly. I made chicken corn soup for Poppa, Bethy, and Laura to heat up for tomorrow's supper, and when Bethy got home I instructed her in how to heat it up. I am so excited!

May 1, 1855

Dear Diary,

Today was finally the Spring Dance at Kirsten's. I
dressed in my dark red dress and draped my lacy shawl over
top. Bethy curled my hair and gathered my tresses in a bun. I
grabbed my hat Poppa gave me, said goodbye to Poppa,
Bethy, and Laura, and dashed out the door to where Jesse
was waiting for me in the wagon.

228

When we arrived at the dance, I could hear music playing from the backyard. Jesse dropped me off at the front door and I hurried inside. Kirsten met me at the door and gave me an enormous hug. I noticed she was wearing the same dress that matched mine. She took my hand and led me outside to where the dancing was taking place. I gasped when I took a look at the yard; it was beautifully decorated with daisies and tulips.

Pretty soon, we both started dancing. It was such a wonderful time. I danced with Scott, Herbert, Hank, Jesse, and Luke! However, later in the day my happiness wavered. Kirsten and I were standing by the punch table, when Cole Brown came over to me. I could still remember his threats to me, and I trembled slightly as he approached.

When he asked me to dance, I politely refused, saying that I was rather tired now. Instead of leaving me be, he said, "Come now, Carolyn. You're not afraid, are you?"

He grabbed me and pulled me into his arms, dancing. My punch spilled all over my dress and the ground. I was too scared to move. What would Cole do next?

Then we suddenly stopped, and I saw Jesse. He said to Cole, "I thought I told you to stay away from my sister?" Then he put a hand on my shoulder and led me away.

Kirsten rushed me inside to her mother, and they worked on getting the stain out of my dress. When the stain was pretty much out, Kirsten and I went back outside to dance some more. I wasn't going to let Cole Brown spoil it!

Jesse and I got home around midnight, but it was well worth it! Poppa was up waiting for us and I told him all about the dance, or as much as I could before I got too tired!

May 4, 1855

Dear Dairy,

Reverend Mast spoke today on how every word of God's is true. Nothing can be altered or changed. But, even though he is this all-powerful God, He will protect us from all evil. Proverbs 30:5-6 says, *"Every word of God proves true; he is a shield to those who take refuge in him. Do not add to his words, lest he rebuke you and you be found a liar."*

May 5, 1855

Dear Diary,

While I was in the kitchen today, I got to thinking about the ball. Not about Cole forcing me to dance with him, but about Jesse. Except for when he rescued me, he seemed to be dancing with Heather Bow most of the night. I wonder if he might like her a little. I remember back in September when we went to the Bows' house for dinner, he seemed rather reluctant to go. I have determined now that that was just an act of shyness!

May 6, 1855

Dear Diary,

During my Bible reading this morning, I came across this verse. Psalm 31:30 says, *"Charm is deceptive, and beauty is fleeting; but a woman who fears the Lord is to be praised."* It is not our outward appearances that make us beautiful, but rather the person we are inside. Does the Lord shine through me? Am I concerned about what people think about me, rather than what the Lord thinks?

May 7, 1855

Dear Diary,

Poppa and Jesse went into town today and when they came back, there was a letter from Cousin George. It read:
Dear Uncle George,
I hope this letter finds you all in good health. I have just

*purchased our tickets and our ship leaves July 3. As of now, it is
just Phoebe and I who will be coming, though Millie is begging our
parents to let her come as well. We shall arrive sometime in
September, and I am assuming that even if you haven't found a
place yet, there will be someplace for us to stay.*

Until September,

George

Poppa told me to write back immediately, telling
George that he would be able to stay with us if we didn't find
anything, but he was looking around. I added that I couldn't
wait to meet Phoebe and see him, and hopefully Millie, again.
I hope he got the hint!

May 8, 1855

Dear Diary,

I am very glad that it is a Saturday today and the girls
could help me do the wash. I must admit, I get quite lonely
when they are not here during the week. While I was tossing
the dirty water into the garden, I saw Jesse bring out the
wagon from the barn into the yard. I thought he was going to
town, and I told him to wait a second and I would get a list.
But he wasn't.

This confused me. "Well, where are you going?"

He just shrugged and left. It was very strange. If he was just going on a ride, why wouldn't he just use his horse instead of the wagon? But instead of trying to figure my older brother out, I just went inside to finish up the laundry.

May 9, 1855

Dear Diary,

Today, Reverend Mast spoke about the love of God, and how he loves us so very much. When God calls us to do something for him, he will help us accomplish it, no matter how hard the task! Romans 8:28 says, "*And we know that in all things God works for the good of those who love him, who have been called according to his purpose.*"

May 10, 1855

Dear Diary,

Jesse went out on his ride with the wagon again right as school was ending. I asked him if he was planning on picking up the girls, but he just shook his head no. Where could he possibly be going?

May 12, 1855

Dear Diary,

I have found out where Jesse has been going! He has been going to the schoolhouse and picking up Heather Bow and taking her home. Laura told me all of this, saying that Jesse parks a little ways from the schoolhouse, and one day, she was wondering where Heather was walking to and she saw Jesse. I told her to keep this news to herself, for I'm sure Jesse wouldn't want this news to be all around town. When Laura left to go outside, I smiled to myself. Heather Bow. I should've thought that's where he was going.

May 15, 1855

Dear Diary,

I needed to get some things at the general store, so Jesse drove me into town. I desperately wanted to bring up Heather Bow, but I was afraid that he would give me the cold shoulder the rest of the day. When we arrived in town, he dropped me off at the store and said he would wait for me outside.

While in the store, I ran into Hank Bow. "Ah, Carolyn, haven't seen you around in a while."

I couldn't help but smile – Hank was always friendly to everyone. Don't get me wrong, I don't like him at all in that way! "Yes indeed. I've been meaning to ask your family over for dinner sometime, but my days keep getting away from me."

He walked with me to the counter and then he said, "You know, I've been seeing Jesse around these past couple days. I think he's sweet on Heather, because he brings her home from school most every day."

I smiled inwardly, "Oh really? That doesn't surprise me one bit."

While we were traveling home, I decided to ask Jesse the question that I've wanted to ask. "Have you seen Heather Bow recently? I've wanted to invite them over for dinner sometime. What do you think?" No answer, so I tried again. "Where have been going on your rides? It must be beautiful to ride around this time of year."

He didn't answer, so I just let it go. If he wanted to be silent, fine. I already knew the truth.

May 16, 1855

Dear Diary,

Reverend Mast spoke today about how God is faithful. He will guard me against Satan and he will deliver me. 2 Thessalonians 3:3, *"But the Lord is faithful. He will establish you and guard you against the evil one."* God will protect me and keep me safe. What a wonderful feeling it is to know that the Lord will never let me down or forsake me!

May 17, 1855

Dear Diary,

It was such a beautiful day today that I decided to go on a walk. As I was walking through the woods, I caught sight of a beautiful patch of wildflowers. Tears gathered in my eyes as I remembered how Momma loved wildflowers. I still remember walking with Momma one day when I was younger. We had just come across a patch of wildflowers and she was leaning down to pick some. "Carolyn, always remember that wildflowers are God's way of making weeds beautiful."

Leaning down now, I grasped the wildflowers and sniffed them. They didn't smell that pretty, but the memories of Momma made up for that. I determined that I was going to put a bouquet on her grave. As I started walking home, I heard a rattling sound. I froze, knowing that could only mean one thing--rattlesnake.

Whipping around, I spotted the rattlesnake a couple feet away. What to do? I shouldn't frighten it but I had to get out of there. I began slowly backing away; never letting my eyes stray from that snake. I was almost out of its line of view. Soon I could run away. But I wasn't quick enough. All of a sudden, the snake lashed out and struck me in my lower leg.

Screaming out in pain, I fell to the ground and the snake slithered away. Pain flooded through my leg and I forced myself to a sitting position. Looking down at my leg, I could see two fang marks. I grabbed my apron and wrapped it around my leg. Telling myself that I had to get home, I forced myself to a standing position. It would be a long journey home, especially since it hurt to put any weight on my foot. I moved from tree to tree, and soon realized that I would never get home.

"Please, God, send help! I need you!" I tried to move again, but eventually just sat down again. The pain was terrible. Tears were streaming down my face. I was scared and I didn't know what to do. I heard a rustling and I tensed up, thinking it was a snake. Cole and Sherry Brown stepped out of the bushes. They looked shocked to find me here. I didn't want to ask them for help, but I did. "Do you think you could help me home? I was bitten by a rattler and I think my leg is starting to swell."

Sherry's eyes widened and I sensed that she was going to help me, but Cole jumped in before she could say anything. "We need to get going. Our mother will be getting worried. You know how mothers are...oh wait, yours died." He left, pulling Sherry along behind him.

I shouted after them, "You can't just leave me here!" But they did. I can't believe he would actually do that to me. I mean, I knew he disliked me, but what he just did was cruel.

My leg was swelling and I had to get home. I decided to try crawling. Perhaps dragging my hurt leg along would work better. It did. I made it to the stream. All I had to do now was cross it. The bridge was farther down the creek, so I decided just to wade through it. I fell down a couple times, and by the time I finally crawled out, I was wet to the bone. Lying down on the ground, I just cried.

How would I possibly make it all the way home? I was exhausted, wet, and my leg hurt terribly. A verse came to me, "*I am with you always, to the end of the age.*" God is always with me. I must remember that. I felt a hand on my shoulder, but then, I blacked out.

When I awoke, Poppa and Aunt Maria were both at my bedside. I looked up at them, "What happened?"

Aunt Maria placed a cool hand on my cheek. "You were bit by a rattlesnake, dear. Luke and Kirsten found you out by the stream." So it was my cousins who found me. Poppa told me to sleep, and so that is exactly what I did.

May 18, 1855

Dear Diary,

Today has been a long day. After lying in bed most of the day, I am ready to get up and do my daily duties. Aunt Maria stayed with me during the day and Bethy came up during the evening. Poppa says I was lucky that Luke and Kirsten came along when they did. The poison was just starting to seep into my bloodstream. God was really watching out for me yesterday.

May 19, 1855

Dear Diary,

I am still stuck in bed today, but Aunt Maria came

over to help with the household duties. I feel so useless when I lie in bed; I feel as though I should be helping. But, whenever I move my foot, the pain reminds me of what happened to put me in the position I am in now. Instead of wasting the time I have, I decided to do some writing in my book.

I wrote down the story about the wildflowers, and I wished dreadfully that I could go back and get them for Momma's grave. But I can't. No matter how much Momma would've liked them, I'm too scared to venture back into the woods to get the wildflowers!

May 20, 1855

Dear Diary,

I'm able to move around some, so Aunt Maria didn't come by today. Poppa helped me downstairs to the couch and told me not to overdo it. Like I would! My foot still hurts when I stand on it for too long a time. After putting leftover soup on to warm, I decided to do some sewing. I do believe that I emptied my mending basket, which is an accomplishment! It just goes to prove that you can do anything if you set your mind to it.

May 23, 1855

Dear Diary,

Poppa allowed me to go to church and I'm so glad he did! Reverend Mast spoke on how if we ask God for something; he will give it to us. He uses the example of wisdom, which I take that as knowledge of something. James 1:5 says, *"If any of you lacks wisdom, let him ask God, who gives to all liberally and without reproach, and it will be given to him."*

After the church service, we had a potluck at church. Of course I didn't bring anything, but Bethy made some raspberry pudding, which I am grateful for. Everyone I saw asked me why I was limping, so I told my snakebite story over and over again. When Mrs. Harp and Mrs. Bow asked me, I elaborated more and told them that I was picking wildflowers for Momma. They seemed to understand why I wanted to do that, for they too remembered that Momma's favorite flower was a wildflower.

In addition to all the friends I saw, I also saw Sherry and Cole Brown at a distance. They didn't come near me, or I them. At one point, I thought I saw Sherry trying to come over and talk to me, but I quickly turned away. I was not in the mood to talk to any of the Browns. So far I haven't told anyone what they did to me, and I'm not sure if I ever will. There is no need to cause trouble when it will only make things worse.

May 25, 1855

Dear Diary,

I was in the kitchen much of the day. I thought my wonderful family deserved a nice cooked meal after a week of leftovers. Around lunchtime, I opened the door to get some more wood for the fire and on the porch lay a bouquet of wildflowers. I was so surprised! Someone had left me wildflowers, and I was sure they were intending for me to put them on Momma's grave. Forgetting all about my chicken and potatoes, I scooped up the wildflowers and headed over to Momma's grave.

Kneeling in the ground beside the tombstone, I laid my hand over top of the mound of dirt. "I don't know who brought these for me. But whoever did, would you let them know that I'm very appreciative? You know I went through lots of trouble trying to get these, and now I have them. They were always going to be for you, Momma." I laid my bouquet of wildflowers on top of her grave. "I love you, Momma."

Then I stood and went back to the house.

May 26, 1855

Dear Diary,

This morning, Jesse questioned me as to why there were wildflowers on Momma's grave, "You haven't gone and picked any, have you, Carrie?"

I shook my head, "Of course not. No, I found them on the porch when I went outside to get wood yesterday. Can you believe it? Someone dropped off wildflowers for me to put on Momma's grave." Jesse got this strange sort of smile on his face, but he went outside without another word on the topic.

May 27, 1855

Dear Diary,

Scott and Jesse went out riding today. I asked Jesse to go by the post office and see if he could mail some letters for me. He shrugged, seeming to say he would try to remember, but I knew he would do it. I was out in the garden when they came riding back. I looked expectantly at Jesse, who said, "All right, I dropped your letters at the post office."

I smiled and turned back around, "Thank you."

But Jesse wasn't finished yet. "Millie wrote to you."

"She did?" I ran over to him and grabbed the letter out of his hand. It has been awhile since I heard from her and I was dying to see if she was coming to America or not. I ran inside, sat on my bed, and read:

Dearest Carolyn,

You won't believe the wonderful news I have! Poppa and Momma have agreed to let me come! After talking about it a long time, they said that helping George and Phoebe and living in America might just be a better life for me. Poppa also said that I did have the money that Farmor gave all the grandchildren after Uncle Philip's death. (Which, was your share of the money ever given to you? I know that is a bit off topic and now I shall return.)

As George has no doubt told you, our ship leaves on July third and then we shall arrive sometime in September. Oh, I am so excited! Doesn't it seem unreal that we will actually see each other before the year ends? I am trying not to dwell on the fact that I am leaving behind Momma and Poppa. I feel deep down that they will come as well, especially once they see how well we are settling.

Phoebe is making this grand list of everything she needs to bring along to set up housekeeping. George told her that we could each only bring one trunk along. I know that shall be hard, so I am going to offer to let Phoebe put some of her things in my trunk. I almost forgot to tell you, George and Phoebe's wedding will be in a few weeks. I shall try and write you about it right before we leave, but I will probably forget like I often do.

I am so excited to see you face-to-face. You will tell Kirsten and your family the good news, right? I'm sure you will. If you are anything like I remember you, you can't keep good news in!

Until we meet again. Love, your dearest,

Millie

I let out a tiny screech of delight. Running over to the window, I stuck my head out. Poppa was talking by the barn with Jesse, Scott, and Mr. Harp. "Poppa!" I shouted out the window. Every face turned my way and I could see Poppa's face etched with alarm. "No, no, it's good news! Millie is coming! Can you believe it? She is really coming!"

I came down from the loft then and ran outside to give Poppa a big hug. While hugging me, he said, "That is wonderful news, my Carrie, though I'm not sure how she convinced my brother to let her come!" It was a happy day for all of us and I can't wait until September when I can finally see Millie again.

May 28, 1855

Dear Diary,

After school let out for the day, I rode over to tell Kirsten the good news about Millie. She was so excited and we screamed, laughed, and cried together. Our circle of friendship would be complete again.

May 31, 1855

Dear Diary,

The news about Millie is so exciting for me, that I almost forgot that I am making a dinner for Jesse's 16th birthday tomorrow. I am making ham, sweet potatoes, beans, squash, and a cake. Aunt Maria is bringing a blueberry pie and *pepparkokor* (gingerbread).

When the girls got home from school, they helped me clean the house and get everything ready for tomorrow's supper.

June 1, 1855

Dear Diary,

While the girls were at school, I did some last minute cleaning and cooking. Once I was sure everything was ready,

I sat down to rest a bit and work on some sewing. Suppertime finally came around and we were able to enjoy a wonderful birthday meal. Jesse received many presents, such as: a carving knife, a straw hat, new shirts, and a pitchfork. He was quite excited by all of his gifts. I couldn't help but think of Momma and how proud she would have been to see Jesse turning sixteen.

I remember one time when I was cooking with Momma and she said, "You children are growing up into such fine and mature adults. I can't wait to watch you grow, physically and also spiritually in the Lord." I started crying, knowing that Momma never would be here to see us, but then I remembered that she can see us. Right now she is up in Heaven with God and can see everything.

June 2, 1855

Dear Diary,

I went on a horseback ride this morning and it felt so free to be out and about. I just love going on rides and exploring God's marvelous creation. It's funny, because I never used to love riding as much as I do now; perhaps it has something to do with Momma's death. She always used to say, "God is everywhere, Carolyn. I can see him in the trees and the birds, the squirrels, and all the animals. I can see him in the sky and the grass. I can see him in you and Bethany, Laura, and Jesse. Don't ever think that God is not with you, for he is very much with you."

June 3, 1855

Dear Diary,

Poppa went into town today and he came back with a letter from *Farmor*. It read:

Dear family,

I suppose that George, Phoebe, and Millie are moving to America. I must say, it sorrows me to no end knowing that I only have two grandchildren left in Sweden. I don't suppose that you will ever come for a visit or move back, for I guess it is much too long of a trip.

On the matter of Philip's money, I appreciate that you have sent such a large amount of money overseas to me, George, but I have decided to split it amongst my grandchildren. The money for Jesse, Carolyn, Bethany, and Laura will be coming with George and Phoebe. I thought it would be safer that way, even though it did arrive safely to me.

There is much excitement happening in planning George

and Phoebe's wedding. To think that this will be the second family wedding you will be missing.

Well, there is much to be done and Melissa has just arrived to talk over some of those details.

All my love,

Farmor

I can't help but get the feeling that *Farmor* would love for us to come and see her. Even if she isn't as personal as *Mormor*, she still loves us a great deal. I know she tells us all that she does so that we will feel bad at not being there and come back, but that shall never happen. America is our home and we are never leaving it.

June 4, 1855

Dear Diary,

Mrs. Bow stopped by today for a visit and at the end of her visit, I invited her and her family for supper on Sunday after church. She seemed very excited to accept just as I was excited to have another dinner. I'm wondering what Jesse will think though.

June 5, 1855

Dear Diary,

The girls and I were busy baking and cleaning today. There is much to prepare in getting ready for a dinner, for I told Mrs. Bow that she didn't have to bring anything! Here is a list of what I'm serving tomorrow:

~ Chicken pot pie

~ Mashed Potatoes

~ Carrots

~ Red Beets

~ Green Beans

~ Strawberry Rhubarb Pie

~ *Frukt* Salad

June 6, 1855

Dear Diary,

After the church service today, the Bows came back to our house and we had a wonderful supper. Mrs. Bow said that I had really outdone myself and Bethy, Laura, and I should be quite proud of ourselves. Throughout the meal, I tried to watch Jesse and see how he was reacting to Heather Bow being so very near. He wasn't doing much, or saying much for that matter, but I could see he was often looking her way whenever he thought no one was watching him. It is quite sweet really, for I do so like Heather and I think she is the perfect person for Jesse!

June 9, 1855

Dear Diary,

This afternoon, Jesse announced that he had to pick something up at the Bow's house in the wagon. Quickly, I asked if I could go along and Jesse just shrugged and said, "Why not?"

Soon we were on our way and when we had reached the Bow's house, Jesse went into the barn. Not sure if I should follow or not, I peeked in to see what they were doing. Huddled in a corner of the barn were Herbert, Hank, and Jesse. As I walked closer, I could see a little cart, not quite as big as a wagon and only for two people, sitting in the corner. When I came to them, I asked who the little cart was for. Jesse said it was ours and I was so excited! Quickly, we loaded it into the wagon, and said good-bye to the Bow brothers.

June 10, 1855

Dear Diary,

Jesse took the cart out for his little ride instead of the wagon and I had a pretty good idea where he went. When he came back fifteen minutes before supper, I was certain he picked up Heather at school and that was the sole purpose of the cart. When I asked him how he liked it, he said it was perfect and changed the subject. Yes, I do believe that my brother is courting Heather Bow, whether he admits it or not.

June 11, 1855

Dear Diary,

Jesse allowed me to hitch Lucia to the cart this morning, and so I rode into town to check the mail. I was so thrilled when I saw a letter from *Mormor* and I just had to read it right away. It read:

Dear Carolyn,

Happy Birthday, my dear girl! I wish I could be there in person to celebrate with you, but alas, I cannot. Your grandpa and I send you all our love and a little gift. It is not much, but I hope you will enjoy it just the same. I shall write a longer letter soon, I just wanted to send you a little note in honor of your birthday.

All my love,

Mormor

I was so surprised. I had forgotten that my birthday was on the fifteenth. Without even thinking, I set the package down on the seat beside me in the cart and tore the box open. Inside I found a beautiful silver necklace and I knew that it was a family heirloom. It touched me so much. If only Momma were here and I could show it to her. I longed for her to be here. This year just hasn't been the same without Momma. I collected myself and rode home to show Poppa my necklace from *Mormor.*

June 12, 1855

Dear Diary,

I have finished my book today! It's the one filled with memories I have of Momma. It is filled with all the stories that Momma has told me over the years and I have even included parts of her diary. I read it aloud to Poppa, Jesse, Bethy, and Laura; their eyes were filled with tears by the time I finished.

Poppa gathered my hands in his and kissed my forehead. "That, my Carrie, is the best way to remember your

Momma." Enveloping the rest of my siblings in his arms, he said, "Your Momma would be so proud of you in the way that you are learning and growing more and more every day. I know I am very proud of you and no matter what, Momma's memories will always be alive in our hearts and our minds."

Now I was crying. His words meant so much to me. There will never be another day like we have just experienced today as a family.

June 13, 1855

Dear Diary,

"*There is a time for everything, and a season for every activity under heaven: a time to be born and a time to die, a time to plant and a time to uproot, a time to kill and a time to heal, a time to tear down and a time to build, a time to weep and a time to laugh, a time to scatter stones and a time to gather them, a time to embrace and a time to refrain, a time to search and a time to give up, a time to keep and a time to throw away, a time to tear and a time to mend, a time to be silent and a time to speak, a time to love and a time to hate, a time for war and a time for peace.*" *Ecclesiastes 3:1-8.*

I think this verse really sums up everything that I have been going through this past year. God is pretty much telling me that there is a time for everything. Everything that happens has a purpose and I know that without God's help, I would've been able to do any of it.

June 14, 1855

Dear Diary,

Well, I've reached the end of my diary. It is still hard to believe that just a year ago Momma gave me this diary as a birthday gift. She told me, "Writing down one's thoughts and feelings is something that helps each person grow. When I was young, I also wrote in my diary. Even today, I will reread that diary and look back at everything that has happened in my life. I learn from my past mistakes and I can relive the special moments."

I have been through a lot this year--death, blizzards, love, harvests, and planting--but I know that whatever may come my way, I will get through it, because I have God to help me.

~ Carolyn Faith Woodsmall

Acknowledgments

God...You are my Savior, my Father, and my shining Prince. You have tuned my heart to you and gave me a pen to write for you. Whenever I would get discouraged or downhearted, you would be there to show me the way. Whenever I was unsure of what move to take next, you were there to point me where to go. You have allowed all of these people to come into my life to help, guide, and critique my book. None of this would have even been possible without You.

Dad & Mom...Thank you so much for all you have done in helping my dream come true. You have stayed up late many nights listening to me talk about what was happening, helping me find an editor, cover designer, and illustrator. You have advised, helped, and encouraged me in this journey and you have taught me to live out my faith. I love you!

Kaitlyn & Jaedyn...You are the best siblings a girl could have! And I'm writing this book hoping that you, your friends, and your peers will have good Christian books to read that will fill your minds with a positive influence. You have read the book and have been so excited for this all to happen.

Autumn...I can't thank you enough! You have made my book come "alive" with your sketches and have spent so much time and effort making them amazing. Every little detail was considered and made to match the description that was in my book. You have read my book numerous times and gave your honest opinion whenever I asked. I am so blessed to call you my friend!

Tracy...Thank you! Thank you! Thank you! Your editing has meant so much to me with all your helpful comments and suggestions, and your mentoring even more!

Steve...I don't even know how to thank you. The cover you designed is absolutely amazing! Your attention to detail and willingness to do so many different designs just to make it look perfect and professional means so much to me. You were so patient with me and you encouraged me not to forsake this book even though school took over my life.

Mrs. Hughes...my 10th grade English teacher...I don't know what to say, I really don't think I would be where I am right now without all that you have taught me. You taught me that editing something numerous times doesn't mean it's bad, it makes it better! You have stretched me and encouraged me to do better because you knew I could. Thank you for everything!

Aunt Emily...You were there to edit my first draft and overwhelm me with all your red marks! You cried when there were sad parts and you were overjoyed when everything worked out right. You have been such an avid supporter and encouragement to me!

My Grandparents...Thank you for getting excited about my book and offering your opinion about what cover to choose! You have gotten so excited about your granddaughter becoming an author and your excitement makes me smile!

Sarah, Moraya, Brooke...Thank you for reading my book and giving me your honest opinion on it. Your words of encouragement have meant so much and I am so blessed to have you as my critics and my friends.

Steve & Shari...You have believed in my book and my dreams and helped me make them a reality. Your support in numerous ways is much appreciated!

The Detweiler family...You have done so much in encouraging me in my writing and pursuing what I want to do. Even in the little things, such as posing for Autumn's drawings and handing out business cards, it has meant so much to me!

Coming Soon!

Discovering Hope

The Diaries of the Woodsmall Sisters

Book Two ~ Bethany's Diary

For updates, visit:

www.woodsmallsisters.com